DESIGN FOR DYING

Also by Anne Morice:

DESIGN FOR DYING

Anne Morice

St. Martin's Press
New York

Library of Congress Cataloging-in-Publication Data

Morice, Anne.
      Design for dying.

      I. Title.
PR6063.0743D47   1988   823'.914   88-1004
ISBN 0-312-01759-6

First published in Great Britain by Macmillan London
Limited.

First U.S. Edition

10 9 8 7 6 5 4 3 2 1

TUESDAY, 17th APRIL

'This one is from Christine,' Aunt Dolly said, planting a pudgy finger on the airmail envelope with the African stamp.

'So it is,' Martha agreed, looking up with a simulated start of surprise from the seed catalogue which had also arrived with the morning post.

'I can't make it out. Why is it addressed to you and not me?'

'Perhaps because the letter inside it is for me?'

'Oh, stuff and nonsense! What would she be writing to you about that she can't say to her own mother? No, don't tell me, I can guess. You've been making mischief again, that's what it is! Going behind my back and whining to Christine that I'm a useless old woman who ought to be put away in an asylum, I shouldn't wonder.'

'Of course not, dear, don't be so silly,' Martha replied, trying to sound amused, although the accusation was close enough to the truth to cause a slight flush to appear on her angular, horsy face and, inevitably, spread from there to the tip of her long nose.

'Then why don't you open it, if you've nothing to hide? Goodness knows, we don't either of us hear from her so often that I'd expect you to shilly-shally about when you do get a letter. Go on, open it, for goodness sake, and let's hear what she has to say.'

'I thought I'd take it upstairs and read it after breakfast.

I haven't brought my glasses down and you know what Christine's writing is like.'

'Then pass it over and I'll read it out to you. I don't need my glasses for that.'

This was true for, although over seventy, Dolly had excellent eyesight, this being one of the few faculties she had retained intact.

'Look out, you're spilling the tea down your dress, Aunt Dolly! Oh dear, what a shame. And I only fetched it back from the cleaners yesterday! Can't you mop it up with your handkerchief?'

'Oh, what's it matter? Gracious, what a bore you are! Sitting there, with that moony expression on your face, nagging on about cleaners' bills when all I want is to hear what Christine has to say. Now then, are you going to allow me to read my own daughter's letter, or aren't you?'

'Oh, look! Here they are all the time!' Martha said, unearthing her spectacles from under the seed catalogue, for if her feeble manoeuvre had failed to divert her aunt's attention from the letter, it had at least provided breathing space in which to weigh up the two evils and to make it plain that the lesser was to keep the letter in her own hands at all costs. She stretched her thin, bony hand across the table for a clean knife and then, with the utmost care and deliberation, slit the envelope. After this, she removed the stamp, in a neat surrounding square of paper, and laid it on one side, explaining that it was for Mrs Bailey's grandson, and all the while visualising the phrases in Christine's scrawly handwriting and imagining how she would skip some of them, paraphrase some and, in the last resort, pretend to find others illegible. She was poor at dissembling and unlikely, she knew, to carry it off with much flair, but it was the best she could think of.

The truth was that several months previously, in a mood

6

of near desperation, she had written to her cousin Christine in very similar terms to those which Dolly had taunted her with, though certainly not hinting that the old woman should be put in a home, for she knew she was incapable of consigning anyone to such a fate. In fact, it was precisely to avoid such a thing that she had appealed to Christine, asking if it might not be possible to provide the money for a nurse, or daily companion, since Dolly's mental state had now deteriorated to a point which made looking after her almost a full-time job. She had also contemplated pointing out that the monthly sum which Dolly contributed to the housekeeping, however fair it might have seemed twenty years before when Christine had sailed to Africa with her first husband, Tim Whitfield, was now totally inadequate. On reflection, though, she had realised that this might merely cloud the issue, for she could envisage Christine seizing on that one point and considering her responsibility ended by upping the allowance with an additional five or ten pounds a month.

That letter had been despatched in January and it was now mid-April. On the assumption that even if Christine were to reply by return, which was unlikely but not to be absolutely ruled out, Martha had reckoned that at least ten days must elapse before she could expect a reply. So as soon as this period was up she began to exercise the utmost vigilance over the incoming mail, going downstairs in her dressing-gown to collect the letters before her aunt was up and ensuring whenever possible that the afternoon's gardening schedule brought her within sight of the front gate at the time of the second delivery.

However, as the weeks went by and no answer came, she had relaxed these precautions and now, some three months later, had been caught off her guard and plunged into the very situation she had most dreaded. She was not in fear of her aunt's displeasure, which she cheerfully endured forty times a day; only of hurting her feelings.

Christine's reply was handwritten on three sheets of airmail paper and even before unfolding it Martha realised with a certain wry amusement that at least it contained no cheque to be explained away.

Adjusting her spectacles and clearing her throat like a nervous lecturer, she skimmed rapidly over the first two paragraphs and almost exclaimed aloud, in a mixture of relief and disappointment, as she realised that no expurgating would be needed either. Her cousin had written as follows:

Dear Martha,

Sorry about the long silence but, as you may have seen in the papers, things have been pretty hectic here, owing to the military coup and curfews and all the rest of it and we've had ghastly staff problems in the house as well as on the plantation. So you needn't think I've been too busy with the social whirl to send any news. As a matter of fact, all that side of life has practically ground to a halt because there are some pretty villainous characters around and most of our friends don't fancy being out after sunset these days. Things are beginning to settle down a bit now, but there have been some really nasty incidents, one of them involving poor old Tim, which gave us all a bad scare, but I'll save the details till I see you. And hold on to your seat because this will probably be some time in August, which brings me to the point of this letter. We've been talking about it for months and Derek has finally decided that the only sensible course is to sell up the estate and leave here before there's another change of government and they bring

8

in those iniquitous laws against taking money out of the country, like we've seen happening in other parts of Africa.

I'm sure you'll understand that we're absolutely heartbroken by the prospect, and it's particularly rough on Derek, being third generation out here and having no family or friends in the UK, unless you count poor old Jim McBean, who retired last year and is now living in some ghastly place like Woking. And I can't say I particularly relish the idea of washing up and scrubbing floors in grey little England. Added to which, it has come at a very awkward moment for Adrian, who is in his third year at the Nairobi school and was hoping to go on to a university in SA. But obviously there's no point in doing that if he can't come here for the holidays, so we'll have to try and squeeze him into a crammers, or something. Or perhaps you know of some local clergyman who could tutor him, if they still do that kind of thing?

Well, it's all very sad and we'll be desperately sorry to leave in so many ways, but it's no good beefing about it because lots of our friends will soon be leaving too and, having made the great decision, I can hardly wait to get away. I'll be able to tell you a lot more about it when we meet, but first and foremost what I'd like you to do is to look around for a suitable house for us. We'd prefer to be somewhere near you, if possible, as I gather your part of Sussex is still reasonably unspoilt, as well as being so convenient for town. Keep in mind that we don't want anything poky, or overlooked by neighbours, but at the same time it mustn't be too vast and rambling, as I'm not eager to spend my whole time doing housework.

Ideally, what we have in mind is a farmhouse

sort of place, with lots of character but completely modernised, with ten or twelve acres, including some rough shooting for Derek. We'll need at least five bedrooms because we're not used to living on top of each other and even though Adrian won't be at home all the time he'll need a place of his own to stack his belongings. I'm a bit out of date with UK prices, but judging by the advertisements in *Country Life* they've shot up like everything else. However, we'd go up to a hundred thousand for something really attractive, so please do your best for us.

Love to Mother and tell her I'll keep all the other news till we meet. We'll have to start off in an hotel in London, unless we have the luck to find someone who can lend us a flat until our stuff arrives, so I'll either cable you our date of arrival, or else ring up when we get there, but don't forget to keep me posted about any possible houses in the mean time.

I must say I'm looking forward to seeing some shows again. Make a note of any you can recommend, as we're probably going to need some guidance.

Yours,
Christine

There was a postscript below the signature, but after one glance Martha kept its contents to herself. Even without it, the letter was not read through with no break, the last paragraph in particular bringing some caustic comments from Martha, who rarely set foot in a theatre and who also had some queries to express concerning the accuracy of the *Country Life* advertisements; but these were mere drops in the ocean compared to the stream of interruptions which flowed from Dolly. Her reactions progressed from excitement to approval and from there to the realms of purest ecstasy. The principal source of delight lay in Christine's specifications regarding the number of bedrooms this unpoky, modernised gem must contain, for she could conceive of no other reason for their requiring so many, except the expectation of being invited to occupy one of them herself.

Although privately agreeing that nothing could be more desirable, Martha nevertheless felt it her duty to dampen these wild hopes, suspecting that they must ultimately be doomed to the most crushing disappointment, but Dolly ignored the warning and continued to rhapsodise on the subject, asking again and again why else, in stating the exact number, Christine had emphasised that it would provide one for each of them.

'I wouldn't set too much store by that, Aunt Dolly. She was probably only trying to give us an idea of the scale of house they have in mind. They may want two spare bedrooms, or she may be planning to get an au pair girl, for all we know.'

'Oh, go on, pour cold water over everything, I should! You're jealous, that's what it is!'

'It sounds as though Tim is staying on, despite the nasty incident, whatever it was,' Martha said, having learnt that a change of subject was often the surest way to dislodge one of Dolly's fixations, even at the cost of putting another one in its place.

'Good thing, too. Best place for him,' Dolly said, rising to the bait.

She had been proud of Tim Whitfield, her first son-in-law, when the young and exceptionally pretty Christine had married him twenty years previously. Even the desolation of knowing that he was to remove her beloved only child

11

half-way across the world had been largely mitigated by the pleasure of boasting about how well he had done for himself to become assistant manager of a vast tea estate, with literally hundreds of workers under him, as well as by the happy anticipation of the many holidays she would be flying out to spend with the young couple.

In the end she had had to wait more than three years before embarking on the first of such trips, which had also proved to be the last, and even this had been cut down from three months to one. She had scarcely arrived in her daughter's house before Christine had discovered herself to be pregnant and, since for some mysterious reason the birth was expected to involve complications, her doctor had advised her to spend the six months preceding it within reach of the finest obstetricians of Nairobi. They had travelled down there together and Dolly had been granted one glorious week before being despatched on the plane back to England and, although there had been talk of future visits and also of Tim and Christine bringing the baby to spend a summer in England, nothing had come of it. Then, when Adrian was two years old, came the news that Christine was divorcing her husband. Six months later she had married Derek Marsh, only surviving member of a family of old established settlers and sole owner of the tea estate where Tim Whitfield was employed.

Evidently, there had been no rancour on either side, for it was clear, even from Christine's scrappy and infrequent letters, that Tim had kept his job and still figured to some extent in her new life. Martha imagined that such close proximity between the old and the new husband must have created a degree of embarrassment, but concluded that the grand colonial house where Christine now lived with Derek Marsh was miles removed, both socially and geographically, from Tim's humbler residence and that in the normal way the two sides were not often obliged to meet.

Dolly, whose loyalties swung about as freely as a sapling in a high wind, had instantly switched allegiance to her new son-in-law, whose wealth and grandeur were on a level to make Christine's former station in life appear quite beggarly by comparison. From that time on, she had never missed an opportunity to scorn and denigrate the lowly Tim, which was rather unfair of her because, as a son-in-law, Christine's second husband turned out to be even more remiss than her first. England was not home for him and when he and Christine went on leave it was always to South Africa or the Seychelles and Dolly had not once been invited to visit them.

On this occasion Martha was content to allow the criticisms of Tim to flow on unchecked, while she cleared away and washed up the breakfast dishes and, as soon as she felt confident that the subject of the impending invasion and the five wonderful bedrooms was temporarily forgotten, she went upstairs to re-read Christine's postscript in the privacy of her own bedroom.

< 2 >

'Come on, now! Don't look so worried. Tell me exactly what the odious creature said and I'll give you the benefit of my opinion,' Avril announced, striking a manly attitude, with her back to the baronial fireplace.

Despite her bossy manner, it was impossible to know Avril well and to dislike her and, although they had little in common, Martha valued her friendship highly, finding something endearing even in her arrogance.

Acquaintances were apt to remark on the many disparities between them, finding it odd that the rich and

13

powerful Avril Meyer should choose to spend so much of her time in the company of a dowdy and impecunious spinster, but Avril viewed the situation differently. She liked Martha and admired what she called her braininess, which made her, second only to herself, the most superior person in the neighbourhood.

'I'd better read it to you,' Martha said, bringing out the letter once more. 'She makes no reference to her mother until right at the end. It begins with another moan about how tough life has become, now that her lot are no longer running things. I needn't bore you with it. Then she goes on to describe the kind of house I'm supposed to conjure up for her. I'll have to answer that part at once and try to get it through to her that she's living in a dream world. She'll think I'm being obstructive, of course, but that can't be helped. She hasn't been to England for over twenty years and obviously the poor girl is completely out of touch with the housing situation. You wouldn't find the sort of place she has in mind for a penny under two hundred and fifty thousand in a neighbourhood like this. If they can only afford to pay less than half of that, they'd better set their sights on Lincolnshire, or somewhere like that.'

'But they definitely want it to be round here?'

'Yes. Near London, you see, but not a whiff of suburbia. She's a fearful snob.'

'Aren't we all? No, not you, I suppose. Could they afford more?'

'Without a doubt, if she's right about their being able to take their money out of the country, and I think she must be, otherwise nothing would have induced her to leave. Anyway, here comes the postscript,' Martha said, turning to the last page and beginning to read aloud: ' "Sorry Mother is being such a bind, but obviously there's no point in trying to sort it out now. We can have a conference when we meet." That's all and it doesn't sound tome as though she had much intention of having Dolly to live with them.'

'On the other hand, she doesn't say outright that she won't,' Avril pointed out. 'It could be that she's at least prepared to share your merry old burden.'

'You don't know Christine,' Martha said gloomily.

'No, and I can hardly wait.'

'You can tell how much affection she has for her mother by the way she wrote, quite apart from the fact that she hasn't been near her for seventeen years.'

'I can sympathise there. I'd prefer not to go near her myself for seventeen years. And one can't tell, Martha; Christine may have mellowed a bit since then. After all, she has elected to live in England, instead of Australia or one of those countries which usually find favour with our ex-colonials.'

'Well, she'd probably consider Australia to be rather common, but it's precisely this sudden urge to come here which makes the problem so very ticklish.'

'How so?'

'Because at least she couldn't completely ignore Dolly's existence, if she were on the spot; but if I write and tell her that it's impossible to find that sort of house at the price she names, it might put her off completely. In fact, that may be just what she's aiming for. She can then shrug it off, opt for South Africa instead and we'd be worse off than ever.'

'Then we won't tell her anything of the kind. We'll find a lovely old half-timbered farmhouse, right next door to Lord Tom Noddy, and she'll be so dazzled that she won't raise a murmur about coughing up the extra hundred thousand or two.'

'Perhaps not, but I'm afraid it would make her even more reluctant to have Dolly on the premises. If only I

15

knew for certain what was going on in her devious little mind it would be such a help, but I do so hate the idea of the poor old woman working herself into a fever of excitement and then getting a terrible let-down.'

'We'll have to clear that fence when we come to it. The first job is to get Christine installed here, so that we can go to work on her.'

'I expect you're right,' Martha agreed, with the hesitancy of a confirmed vacillator faced with two equally disagreeable choices and hoping to remain uncommitted to both. 'Although the sort or properties she has in mind are pretty thin on the ground, at any price,' she added on a more hopeful note.

'Then we'll have to see what can be done by bribery, corruption, blackmail and influence. I'll ask Billy Jones to keep his eyes peeled for any snips which may be coming on the market. Don't worry, Martha, I shall take the whole thing in hand.'

And Martha sighed again, realising that this was all too likely to be true.

< 3 >

Extract from Dolly Kershaw's letter to Mrs Alice Barnby:

   . . . wasn't it a hoot? You should have seen her face! I could hardly stop myself from laughing out loud. Of course, the silly creature hasn't an inkling that I've seen through her sly tricks. Sometimes I believe you think I'm exaggerating, but many's the time I've caught her sneaking downstairs for the post when she imagined I was fast asleep. What could I do, though? Have it out with her would be your way, I know, but she can be a terror when she's roused and she'd only have denied it. I did once ask the postman about an airmail letter, pretending I couldn't remember whether it was last week it had come, or the one before, but he just gawped at me, as though I were mad, so I expect she'd got round him in some way. And I haven't liked to say too much about it to Christine. She's got worries of her own, poor girl. Besides, what would be the use? You-know-who is always fidgeting around when she sees me writing a letter, and offering to take it to the post for me, in her smarmy way, though she's keen enough to push me out for a walk at other times, so I expect half my letters don't get posted at all.

Anyway, I caught her red-handed this morning. She tried her utmost to keep me in the dark, but I was too quick for her and in the end she had to give in. So now everything's going to be all right and life begins again! I'm so thrilled I feel like dancing a jig, but I have to be careful not to show it, otherwise she'll find some way to pay me out. Anyway, she's not here now. Gone off to see the stuck-up Lady Avril she's so fond of kowtowing to. So I'm up here in my room, having a little private celebration on my own, with a nice bottle of sherry, which I popped out to the grocers for as soon as the coast was clear. I nearly came a cropper over that, though, because I'd forgotten it was Mrs Bailey's day and I ran straight into her as I came in the front door. So of course she wanted to know where I'd been and whether she could take my parcel for me, and all the rest of it. You can't think how awful it is being spied on like this and that woman gets more bolshie every day. I

17

could laugh when I think about it, though, because
Martha most likely won't be able to afford her two
mornings a week when she hasn't got my money coming in every month, and that'll serve them both right.
Still, I shouldn't be catty, should I, on this happiest
of all days?

Well, dear, do drop me a line and let me know
how you're getting on in good old Eastbourne and
as soon as we're all settled in the new house we
must fix a date for you to come and stay. Christine
and Derek are planning to have quite a grand estab-
lishment, by the sound of it, so there'll be plenty of
room for you. No cheese-paring with those two, I can
promise you . . .

< 4 >

'Your friend, Avril, is on the war-path again,' Miranda
Jones announced, tripping into the studio and osten-
tatiously picking her dainty way through the debris of
books and files and periodicals which littered the floor
between the door and the drawing-board, where her father
was at work.

He was an ugly, gangling man in his middle forties,
with a lopsided smile, fine, silky hair like a baby's and
so short-sighted that his nose was almost brushing the
drawing-board. His voice was soft, high-pitched and
rather pedantic, characteristics which were reflected in
his elegant handwriting and in the delicacy and precision
of his designs. Every other appurtenance, including his
clothes, was shabby, uncoordinated, or badly in need of
a good brush, which was exactly the way he liked it.

Miranda, who was seventeen, small-boned, but on the

plump side, did not resemble her father in the least. In her view, it was marginally the less of two evils, but in fact she took after her mother, a brunette beauty who had started life as an actress and, finding small pleasure in matrimony and motherhood, had rapidly abandoned both, in order to take up residence with a woman friend in Provence.

Miranda had also recently left home, in her case to join a ballet school and set up with three other girls in a flat in Battersea, but she invariably returned for weekends and holidays. On these occasions Billy, who was a kindly man, bore with her masterful ways and passion for the uncluttered scene with as much patience as he could summon, only rarely permitting himself to retreat to his studio in the garden and shake all over. Whenever Miranda violated the unwritten law and invaded this privacy, which happened rather frequently, he became momentarily rigid with irritation, shutting his eyes and mouthing silent phrases, as though entreating himself not to strangle her.

'How do you know about Avril?' he asked now in a low voice, having got himself together again after one of these convulsions.

'She rang up. Going on like nobody's business. I said I'd tell you.'

Some people, clients in particular, were persistent campaigners for a telephone to be installed in Billy's studio, but Avril was not one of them. Aware that it had been constructed as far away from the house as possible for the express purpose of being out of earshot of the telephone bell, she was careful to time her calls to coincide with Miranda's visits.

'What did she want, do you know?' Billy asked mildly, quite in control again.

'Yes, of course I do. We're not all as potty as you, darling. I should think you'll be pleased, actually. She's got a terrific conversion job lined up for you. She'll be round with the details this evening, but she told me to warn you to be ready to drop everything and get to work on it, as from tomorrow.'

'Oh, is that all? What a relief! I was afraid you were going to say that someone had dropped out and she wanted me to go to dinner. But that's all right. I've only got the Parish Council's plans for the cricket pavilion at present and I dare say they're in no particular hurry. You can ring Avril back some time and say that as long as she doesn't arrive here during working hours her word is my command.'

'I expect she knows that by now. Do you want to hear some more about it?'

'Well, no, I'd rather not, if you don't mind. I'd only have to hear it all over again from her, which would be very boring.'

'All right, then, I'll just give you the outline,' Miranda said relentlessly. 'Then you can think about it while you're working. You remember Bookers Farm?'

'No.'

'Yes, you do. Avril took us to see it on Boxing Day, when she and Robert first got the idea of buying it and farming the land with theirs. There were a lot of bantams wandering around and some half-witted children. You must remember?'

'If you insist. Is that what I'm to convert?'

'Yes, but not for the children and bantams. Apparently, Robert was stuck with them as sitting tenants, so he took the man on as cowman, but he was absolutely dead lazy and useless. So now he's wangled a council house for them and the farm is empty. Avril says it's in a revolting state and she wants you to tart it up and fling on a few extra rooms and then she'll get a fancy price from these people who've been living abroad somewhere. Only she says you'll have to work fast because it's vital to push through the planning permission at their next meeting.'

'Which is when?'

'In a month's time.'

Recognising that he was committed to hearing the whole saga, whether he wished to or not, Billy opened his eyes and applied himself once more to the south elevation of the cricket pavilion, allowing about one-quarter of his mind to follow Miranda's narrative, which had now moved into speculations about the family Avril had marked down as purchasers. She could not remember their name, but it gradually emerged that they were related in some way to Martha Kershaw. It was only at the second mention of Africa that things clicked into place and he laid down his pencil and gave her his full attention.

There were no other visible reactions, however, for it was only the pinpricks of life which set his nerves on edge. Shocks of the thunderbolt variety usually left him relatively unmoved and he allowed his daughter to finish her tale without interruption.

When it was over and he was alone again at last he moved away from the drawing-board and squatted down beside the lowest shelf of his bookcase. Unlike his wife and daughter, who prided themselves on their orderliness and could never find what they were looking for, Billy could invariably pick out any article from its surrounding chaos at a moment's notice and in no time at all he had his hands on an old photograph album, which had been tucked away for years between a Guide Bleu and the Collected Works of Lord Byron.

He settled himself comfortably on the floor and began slowly and methodically to turn over the thick grey pages, passing his magnifying glass up and down until it hovered

21

and finally came to rest over a faded snapshot of three young people dressed in summer clothes and posed against a background of the steps of the Madeleine. The central figure was a girl in a billowing ankle-length skirt and she had an arm round each of her male companions. One of them was an overgrown, bespectacled youth with wispy, flyaway hair, and the other a stocky, dark-haired boy, with a horizontal grin so wide that it had the effect of splitting his face in half. The caption underneath said simply: 'Chris, Tim, Self'.

Billy studied it for a while, then shut the album, leaving it on the floor, before returning to his drawing-board to add a couple of Corinthian columns to his cricket pavilion.

FRIDAY, 3rd AUGUST

The hotel was just round the corner from Harrods and the reunion had been fixed for twelve-fifteen in the Waverley Bar. Martha purposely arrived ten minutes late because, as a girl, Christine had been notoriously unpunctual and it was hard to believe that her subsequent life had done anything to cure this habit. Moreover, hotels, even quite modest ones, were apt to throw her into a panic of shyness and hotel bars were the worst of all. She could never decide whether to march boldly up and ask for what she wanted, or to wait discreetly at a table until someone came to take her order, whether to pay now or later, how much to tip and whether the request for a bitter lemon would be met with supercilious looks and directions to another part of the building.

By delaying her arrival she hoped to avoid all these hazards and to find Derek, at least, waiting to greet her. She had never met him, but Christine had sent photographs at the time of their marriage and, even if he had shrunk a little in fourteen years, she felt sure he would still tower over most other people and stand out from them by sheer bulk.

It was therefore a setback to discover that the bar contained no one at all of that description and she was about to retreat and nerve herself to make some enquiries at the reception desk when she noticed that a stocky, middle-aged man, with frizzy grey hair, who had been sitting alone in a far corner, was now on his feet and waving to her. She did not recognise him until, thrusting chairs aside with both hands, he came towards her, his face split horizontally into the familiar wide smile, and she realised that he was Tim Whitfield.

'Hallo, Martha! It is Martha, isn't it? I think I'd have known you anywhere. You've hardly changed at all.'

She saw at close quarters that he had not either. He was still the same old hearty, rather obtusely good-natured man whom she remembered of old and to Martha, whose early reading had included weekly instalments of a jolly character called Tiger Tim, the old nickname was still just as appropriate.

'Neither have you really, Tim. It's just that I wasn't expecting you.'

'No? Well, the others will be along presently. Derek had to go and talk business with some bwanas in the City and Christine's dragged Adrian off to buy his clothes for school. She'd got a list as long as your arm, poor girl, but she said she'd do her damnedest to be back by twelve-thirty. Now, what's your tipple?'

Having stated her choice and refused to be argued out of it, Martha was somewhat mortified to see him raise his arm aloft and click his fingers to attract the waiter's attention. Evidently, the waiter wasn't too thrilled about it either, but he maintained a frigid calm as he took the order for another of the same and one tomato juice.

'And bring us a dish or two of nuts and what-have-you, there's a good lad,' Tim added, oblivious of the unfavourable impression he was creating. He then turned back to Martha. 'Now, bring me up to date. How's life? How's my poor old ex-mother-in-law, for a start?'

'Poorer and older, I'm afraid. Like the rest of us.'

'Oh, come off it! I told you, you've hardly changed at all. Hair a bit grey, of course, but then so's mine. You

24

wait till you see Christine, though. She's a marvel. Put on a few pounds here and there, but otherwise she doesn't look a day older.'

The complacency with which he made this boast smacked so strongly of the proud, uxorious husband that Martha seriously began to wonder if one of them was insane. It actually passed through her mind that she and Dolly were nothing but a pair of old lunatics, feeding each other's fantasies and between them fabricating the entire story of Christine's divorce and remarriage. However, she had not yet sunk so low in her own estimation as to doubt that she had heard Tim refer to his 'ex-mother-in-law' and, partially reassured by this, she said evenly, 'Well, it's a nice surprise to see you again, Tim, after so many years. Do you know, I hadn't even taken it in that you were coming to England? But perhaps it wasn't possible for you to stay on, once the estate had been sold?'

'Well, no,' he replied, looking faintly puzzled. 'There was never any question of that. What I mean is, experienced old hands like me are still needed and they offered me a five-year contract, as it happens, but I wasn't interested, thanks all the same. Not that they were bothered. They'll find plenty of other chaps only too keen to take it on. Russian or Chinese, I shouldn't wonder. Don't look so shocked, Martha. I'm not quite so cynical about it as I pretend and I've nothing to complain of. I've had a good life out there and now it's over. I can't honestly say I ever expected to be redundant at my age, but that's the luck of the draw. No good grumbling.'

'And now that the break has come, or been forced upon you, do you mean to settle in England too?'

He glanced at her enquiringly, as though not quite hearing what she had said, then looked quickly away again, his face creasing into the wide smile.

25

'Oh, look! Here comes Chris! Not too full of the joys of spring either, judging by her expression. Over here, Chris, old girl,' he called, semaphoring with both arms.

It was true that except for a little stoutness round the waist and hips she was essentially unchanged. Neither time nor experience had left any visible mark, or removed any of the bloom. She still had the same copper-coloured hair, the same radiantly healthy skin, slim legs and ankles and the same capacity to make Martha feel like a carelessly assembled scarecrow. Moreover, her clothes, although obviously split new, were an exact replica of the regulation outfit of her youth: brown and white tweed suit, cashmere jumper, double row of pearls and real crocodile shoes.

'Phoof! Much too hot,' she complained, sinking into a chair and flapping a doeskin glove, having flashed both sides of her face within an inch of Martha's, by way of cousinly greeting. 'I shall really have to get some summer dresses somehow or other this afternoon. That shop over the road looks quite promising.'

'I should have thought you'd have plenty of that sort of thing in your luggage.'

'I have, but not with me. Most of the stuff is coming by sea. I just picked up a few things in Nairobi to tide me over, but I'd forgotten the sun could occasionally shine in this benighted country. Honestly, isn't London hell? The noise! And the dirt! I don't know how you stand it.'

'I don't have to very often.'

'Don't blame you. How's Mother, by the way?'

'Fair. She has her good days.'

'Well, that's a relief.'

'And her bad.'

'Oh, really? Well, you must tell me about it over lunch. I've booked a table for us in the restaurant at one-thirty. Derek should be back by then. There was a great fuss

26

about finding a table for five in the window, but they climbed down in the end. But listen, Martha, there's something I want to get organised before Adrian appears. I'm sure it's not your fault, but there's been a muddle about our hotel rooms.

'What's wrong with them?'

'Nothing, as far as they go. It's simply that when we arrived last night they told us they'd only reserved three rooms, instead of four, as I'd particularly asked. And now they have the cheek to tell me that we can't have another until the end of the week because they're booked solid.'

'I'm sorry, Christine, but . . .'

'My dear, I'm perfectly certain it's they who have bungled it because I remember so well my telling you it was essential that we each had a room of our own. You haven't met Derek yet, but you'll understand when you do, and I absolutely refuse to double up with him for another five days. He's so enormous, poor darling, it's like sharing a room with a baby elephant.'

'Well, you see, Christine, I . . .'

'My dear, do please get it through your head that I'm not blaming you in the least. Goodness knows, I appreciate everything you've done more than I can say. Finding the house was a marvellous piece of luck. It sounds absolutely right for us and I can't wait to see it. The amazing thing is that everyone has been telling me the most appalling tales about inflationary prices over here, but obviously they were wildly exaggerated.'

'Well, perhaps not altogether. This one happens to be rather exceptional.'

'Oh, I'm not underestimating you for a moment. And that friend of yours deserves a medal. What's her name? Lady Meyer?'

'Lady Avril Meyer, if you want to be pernickety.'

'Oh, I see. Well, you must let me have her number, so that I can ring up and thank her. But, to get back to the immediate problem, what am I going to do about this extra room?'

'The thing is, Christine, why is it so absolutely essential to have all four rooms in the same hotel?'

'Well, because of Adrian, of course. You can't have forgotten Adrian?'

'Certainly not, but . . .'

'What's happened to the boy, by the way?' Tim interrupted. 'Wonder what he's up to?'

'He's in his room. He blackmailed me into buying him the most wickedly expensive tape-recorder and record-player and, of course, he can't wait a minute to try them out. I do hope he doesn't fuse the entire building.'

'I think I'll go and seek him out. It might be a good idea if he and I shunted off somewhere for lunch on our own.'

'Oh no, really, Tim, you don't want to drag about looking for restaurants in this heat; 'specially after all the trouble I've been to getting a table for all of us here.'

'All the same, old girl, I think it might be better if Adrian and I made ourselves scarce. I know you and Martha want to have a natter and we can all meet up again this evening before the theatre. So I'll say goodbye, Martha. Give my regards to Dolly and we'll be seeing you both next week, no doubt.'

'Good old Tim being tactful,' Christine said, winking at Martha as he hurried away. 'Or cowardly,' she added on a more thoughtful note.

'Why cowardly?'

'Because it may have begun to dawn on him, just as it's already dawned on me, that you don't understand at all about the way we live and I suppose he was afraid that

28

when the penny dropped you might disapprove.'

'He needn't have worried. I think it's finally beginning to dawn on me and I must say it explains a lot. The reason for so many bedrooms is because the caravan, as well as Derek and Adrian, also includes your ex-husband?'

'And I take it from your prissy expression that you do disapprove?'

'No. It's not an arrangement that would appeal to me, personally, but that's neither here nor there. Perhaps I should warn you, though, that your mother has not yet quite caught up with the permissive society.'

'So what?' Christine said. 'She'll come round to the idea eventually and, if she doesn't, I couldn't care less. I've no intention of leading my life to suit her. I'm forty-five, believe it or not.'

'Why should I not? I was twelve when you were born.'

'Is that all? Somehow, I always thought of you as middle-aged even when I was a child.'

'Thanks.'

'Oh, no offence, my dear. I suppose I was a bit in awe of you, really. You were supposed to be the clever one, I remember. All that talk about you going up to Oxford and everything. Though you never made it, did you?'

'Only for one term. Then my mother died. My father was an invalid, as you may also recall. He couldn't afford a nurse, so I had to come home.'

'Yes, I do remember. And no sooner had Uncle Wilfred been gathered than my wretched old mamma landed herself on you. Poor old Martha! Can't have been much fun. Still, I suppose it's better than being all alone in your old age.'

'Which certainly doesn't seem to be the fate which is

in store for you. Tell me, Christine, how long has this ménage à trois been going on?'

'Oh, ages. From the beginning, in fact.'

'You mean you took your ex-husband along on the honeymoon?'

'Still the same old sarcastic Martha! No, it wasn't quite like that. There was a bit of what you might call awkwardness at the start. It took Tim a while to come round to our way of thinking, but it was all so ridiculous. Quite apart from the fact that he and Derek had to meet almost every day in the office, the three of us had always hit it off so frightfully well. We'd done everything together. Well, you know, practically everything. Just because Derek and I happened to fall in love there was no reason why we shouldn't continue just as before.'

'I can see that some people might consider it a reason.'

'What do I care? Life's too short to worry about conventions. Besides, it made it so much nicer for Adrian to have us all under one roof.'

'Yes, it doesn't really quite rate as a broken home.'

'Which reminds me, Martha. I was going to ask if you would mind having Adrian to stay for a few days? It would solve this hotel problem and of course we'd pay you something towards his keep. He'd be no trouble, I promise you, and I'd be ever so grateful.'

Martha demurred a little, pleading the smallness of her cottage as an excuse to refuse, and pointing out that Adrian would be uncomfortable, as well as bored to death, but she knew from the start that it was a waste of time. Christine had always got her own way and the record showed that she had not changed. It was entirely typical of her that, so far from shedding the responsibility of one of her relatives, the interview ended with Martha's taking on an extra one.

TUESDAY, 7th AUGUST

Dolly had got into the way of visiting the building site almost every day, driving the workmen into sullen furies with her complaints about their laggardliness and the number of empty milk bottles they left lying around. It was her new absorbing hobby and when she could not prevail upon Martha to drive her there she would hire Lubbock, the local taxi owner, to do so instead. Accusations of extravagance were met with 'Heigh-ho, in for a penny, in for a pound' and suchlike fatuities, which was clever thinking, for it meant that Martha nearly always did drive her. Experience of Christine's methods and Lubbock's hiring rates told her that 'Heigh-ho, in for a penny and in for a fiver' would have been nearer the mark.

A still heavier burden of guilt lay in the relief which she personally gained from Dolly's being so happily occupied in her fool's paradise, causing her to absent herself for long periods of the day and usually to return home so invigorated that she was ready to eat up her supper with none of the usual complaints, and then 'Heigh-ho for an early night!'

So Martha stifled her conscience as far as she could by turning herself into a voluntary taxi service and tried hard to quash the hope that things might go on in this way for ever and ever.

Needless to say, they could not. Resentment was building up into a solid wall of hostility between the builders and Dolly and the last straw was piled on when she accused one of them of attempting to steal an ancient iron fireback which had been unearthed from behind a bricked-up fireplace and later been mysteriously transferred to an outhouse. The fact that he had been intending to steal it in no way diminished his burning indignation and Cafferty, the foreman, complained to Billy Jones.

Billy, for whom any direct contact with Dolly was painful, passed the complaint on to Avril, and her brand of oil for these troubled waters was labelled Patience. She recommended all concerned to hold their horses for a few days, since Mrs Marsh would shortly be arriving in the neighbourhood and, by all accounts, was more than capable of keeping her mother in order.

Billy was not so sanguine. He maintained that Christine's filial affection even fell short of that.

'You must remember, Avril, that she went to Africa, in the first place, for the sole purpose of putting a continent between herself and her mother, so it's not very likely that she means to have much to do with her, now that she's come back.'

'You have the same defeatist attitude as Martha,' Avril said. 'And I was under the impression that she went to Africa because she had married Tim Whitfield.'

'No, I think it was the other way round,' Billy said.

'And I think you're biased.'

'We'll just have to hope for the best,' he muttered, pretending not to have heard her last remark. 'And perhaps the mere fact of her choosing this neighbourhood is a promising sign.'

'I must warn you that Martha has a rather different explanation for that.'

'Has she? What?'

'That Christine's motive in coming here is to carry on

with her threesome without becoming a social outcast. She's got it into her head that we're such a sophisticated lot that we're more likely to accept the situation without a blink than the inhabitants of Lincolnshire or New South Wales.'

'Indeed? And what was Martha's reaction to that?'

'I believe she warned the silly creature that even our decadent society might not be quite prepared for that kind of set-up for the middle-aged. But it gives us a lever, don't you think? Either she takes Dolly in hand, or we'll all make a pact to cut her dead in the village. On the other hand, we might do better to work through the husband.'

'Which one?'

'The new one, Marsh. Martha says that, on the surface, he's completely under Christine's thumb, just like all the other men in her life, naming no names. Apparently, she was going on all through lunch about how impossible it was to make any arrangement about her mother until they were settled in the new house and all the great booby could say, in effect, was "yes, dear," "no, dear".'

'Well, that doesn't sound very promising.'

'Ah, but it seems that after lunch it was a different story. Christine bustled off to do some shopping and this Marsh seized on Martha and gabbled in her ear that he'd arranged for his Bank to pay five thousand pounds into her account immediately, plus a hundred a month until such time as they came to some definite decision as to where Dolly was to live. He also cautioned her not to mention any of this to Christine, as she was rather scatter-brained about money, which you'll agree is a novel way of putting it.'

'So Martha is to be bought off, is she?'

'Better than a slap in the eye with a wet fish, don't you think? She'll be able to afford a decent car at last and probably have Mrs Bailey an extra couple of days. Besides, Martha's such a saint, you know. She doesn't resent the old woman half as much as you or I would. No, I see it as a very promising development.'

'I doubt if it will satisfy Dolly, though. It's all too clear that she's firmly set on going to live in Christine's lovely new house and nothing will shake her out of it.'

'She'll be in her grave before it's completed, if she goes on upsetting the builders. God help us if Cafferty should really take umbrage,' Avril remarked thoughtfully. 'He can be a very hot-tempered man, as we both know. Still, there's nothing much to be done about it at present. Smooth him down as best you can and we should be able to get through the next few days without a crisis.'

< 2 >

Extract from Adrian Whitfield's letter to his friend, Diana Moore:

. . . grotty little cottage, where I have to sleep in a rotten camp bed in the dining room because there was No Room at the Inn! There was some muddle about the bookings and after two nights I was turfed out. Very super place, though. Make sure your parents book in there when they come over. Any developments there, by the way? If they do decide to make it for Christmas I'll be able to escort you to some of the hip places I discovered when I was in London. Incidentally, as far as I've been able to gather, hip is still an in word, but I'll investigate this vital matter and let you know!!! I expect the first thing that will

34

hit you about London is seeing so many white people in the streets. Absolutely millions of them. It's rather weird until you get used to it.

A worse shock for me, though, was meeting my ghastly relatives. You remember how my mother used to make us hoot with laughter with stories about my eccentric grandmother? She sounded quite good fun and I was rather looking forward to seeing her in the flesh, but she's not a bit like that now she's old. Honestly, Di, she's absolutely barmy and completely sloppy and disgusting. She spills food all over herself and she's always practically setting the place on fire and forgetting to turn the gas off. Grotty in the extreme. I wouldn't be surprised if she hits the bottle actually. She absolutely pongs of it sometimes.

And the other one is nearly as bad. I've been told to call her Aunt Martha, and I must say it absolutely suits her down to the ground, although she's actually my cousin once removed, or something, the daughter of my late lamented great uncle, if you can work all that out, and she looks as if she'd been buried and dug up again. I hope this isn't putting you off!!! As you know, my parents are relatively sane and there are no hereditary taints to worry about with my stepfather, thank God, so the chances don't look too grim for our children, if we have any!!!

Anyway, with luck I'll be out of this dump in a day or two because my parents are coming down to stay at a place called the Beresford Court Hotel, which is about three miles from the new house. Did I tell you in my last that we've definitely decided to buy it and move in as soon as it's ready? I've got an absolutely smashing bedroom, with a bathroom next door. There's only one crummy little downstairs bathroom at present, but we're having three more put in. The architect had only allowed for two, but my stepfather made him alter the plans to make another one and I must say I agree with him for once.

Apart from the decorating, they think the work will be finished in another few weeks, so it ought to be habitable by the time you come over for Christmas, if you do (there's a spare room connecting with mine, which is one of the most smashing things about it!!!!).

Actually, I spend quite a lot of time there now. It's better than sitting around doing nothing in this dump and the foreman's quite a decent chap, even though he does call me Sonny. We've had some quite interesting talks. His father was a game-keeper, it seems (although not much like Lady Chatterley's, by the sound of it!) and he's got some good stories about various poachers he knew as a boy. He even lets me help with a few jobs from time to time, although he made me swear not to let on to his union (I think this was meant to be a joke!).

Well, darling Di, I can't wait to see you. Roll on Christmas . . .

< 3 >

For once in her life Avril's confidence was misplaced and a crisis of a kind occurred within a few hours of her conversation with Billy, although whether the removal of a section of floor-boarding, which caused all the trouble, had been motivated by malice remained a matter for their private conjecture.

It was certainly an unfortunate coincidence that the

square hole in the floor should have been just inside that very room which, as all the work-team were sick of hearing, Dolly had earmarked for herself; but, as Cafferty pointed out, that piece of flooring was riddled with dry rot and its replacement was clearly scheduled on the plans.

When Billy gently remonstrated that the door should have been locked, or at least had some warning posted on it, he fully agreed that this was so, but then on the other hand the new timber for the floor was to have been delivered that very morning, but by some ill chance had failed to arrive, giving him no alternative but to switch the men over to another job, and this small precaution had been overlooked. It was a terrible business, but how was he to know the old lady would go poking about up there on her own, when hadn't he warned her a thousand times that she was putting herself at risk?

She was not gravely injured, but her left arm was fractured and her face bruised. Furthermore, the shock induced a mild heart attack and she was subsequently inclined to be hysterical. It was the last symptom, more than any other, which persuaded the doctor to advise a stay in hospital, where she had been taken for x-rays and emergency treatment, for he knew from long association with the patient that the hysteria might continue indefinitely while she was in Martha's care, but was likely to ease off sharply under the steely eye of Matron.

Stricken with guilt and remorse, both on account of her new affluence and for having so neglected her charge, Martha insisted that she be given a private room. This order was instantly countermanded by Christine, who arrived the following morning and demanded the patient's transfer to the public ward, explaining to everyone who had time to listen that poor Mum would be so much happier in the cheerful company of other sufferers than stuck away on her own. Later, in the privacy of their suite at the Beresford Court Hotel, she requested Derek to tell her where the hell Martha imagined the money was coming from to pay for such luxuries and whether he did not agree that, being now forced to make their home in the ghastly welfare state, they might at least get something out of it?

Both questions were more or less rhetorical, so he was not obliged to answer them, which may have been just as well, for within twenty-four hours Christine had reversed all her opinions and come out strongly on Martha's side. Her excuse for this was that she had by then acquired first-hand experience of the discomforts and petty restrictions of the public ward, would not tolerate them for any member of her family and blow the expense! In reality, though, the change of heart sprang from rather different causes. Having, through lack of practice in observing other people's rules, arrived at the hospital a good half-hour before visiting time and been refused admittance, she had flung her weight about to such an extent that it had finally been necessary to pacify her with a cup of tea in Sister's private cubby-hole. During this interval she had been dismayed to learn that she need have no fears for her mother, as the surest remedy for elderly patients lay in their own incentive to get well. Now that Mrs Kershaw was enjoying the delightful prospect of moving into her daughter's beautiful new home and was thus an object of envy to every other inmate of the ward, there was nothing to hold her back. To know that Dolly was romancing on in this strain to Martha and Mrs Bailey was one thing; spreading her foolish fantasies round the entire neighbourhood through the medium of Women's Surgical was quite another, and even before the first visitors came surging through the swing doors Dolly found herself being trundled back to her private room.

Only one explanation for her departure occurred to the onlookers, and Cafferty, paying a duty visit to his mother-in-law, who had dislocated her shoulder while rescuing his fifth child from certain death by defenestration, was disgusted to learn that funny old Mrs Kershaw had now been discharged.

FRIDAY, 10th AUGUST

One thing was certain: if the silver lining existed, Christine could be relied upon to snatch it with both hands. No sooner had she settled her mother's hash than she telephoned Martha to suggest that Adrian should stay on at the cottage so long as Dolly remained in hospital. Apart from there being plenty of room for him now, it would be much more suitable than mooning around in the hotel.

'I can't see much difference between mooning there and mooning here,' Martha protested.

'All the difference in the world, my dear. For one thing, you'll be able to keep an eye on him and see that he buckles down to some work. He's got dozens of books he's supposed to get through before term starts and, so far as I know, he hasn't opened one of them. All he wants to do is play about with those tapes and things. I really haven't time to keep chivvying him, and besides he'd probably take more notice of you. And I'm sure you can find ways of making him useful. You have my full permission to give him as many jobs as you like.'

'That's most generous of you, Christine, but it doesn't sound like a very exciting prospect for Adrian.'

'Oh, it won't hurt him, it's high time he came out of the clouds and discovered how the other half lives. In any case, I couldn't have him back here until after tomorrow. I've got to spend the day in London.'

'But you've only just come out of London.'

'I know, but some of the clothes I bought needed alterations and I don't trust that shop to get it right. I'm going to have some fittings.'

'How will you go? By train?'

'No, car. We've hired one from that man, Lubbock, you put us on to. I'll probably have a mass of parcels, so it'll be much more convenient than the train. Tim says he'll drive me up.'

'Oh, I see.'

'Derek was going to, but he's got to have a conference with Billy about the house. You know we agreed to pay for all the fixtures and fittings, as well as the decorating? I prefer to, really, because we can choose our own colours and so on, but I can't describe to you what the firm Billy found for us are proposing to charge. Out of this world! The whole thing has got to be hammered out and tomorrow is the only time Billy has free. So Tim offered to take me instead. To be perfectly frank with you, Martha, I'm a bit nervous of driving on English roads, and I haven't a clue about these parking meter things.'

'You do realise that tomorrow is Saturday and everything will close down at one o'clock?'

'Of course I do, I'm not as backwoodsy as all that. But we thought we might stay up and have lunch in town and go to a show. Which reminds me, Martha; if you've got nothing special on, would you feel like giving Derek lunch and running him back to the hotel afterwards? I'd be ever so grateful. He won't have a car, you see, but he can easily walk across to you from Billy's house. Would you mind awfully? I tell you what, I'll bring you a nice present from London, something really glamorous.'

'There's no need. I expect you'll have enough parcels without that.'

'Well, anyway, I'll ring you as soon as I get back. And

41

don't forget what I said about Adrian. Actually, it's just struck me; you'll probably be glad of his company. He can be quite forthcoming, with a little encouragement, and it'll be nicer for you than being entirely on your own.'

< 2 >

Martha had not thought of Adrian in quite those terms, for although he had inherited his mother's colouring, he was sadly lacking in self-assurance. He was an undersized, surly youth with a spotty complexion, and her diffident attempts to establish a rapport had not so far struck a responsive note. She guessed that he was by nature shy and self-conscious, realised too that he must be bored to death and sympathised accordingly; but when she had tried to alleviate his situation by offering to invite her young friend, Miranda Jones, over for supper one evening he had given her a glassy look, said 'No, thanks,' and immediately resumed his study of the evening's television programmes.

She had accepted the snub without rancour, concluding that he was still too immature to feel any stirrings of interest in girls.

Reconsidering the matter in the light of Christine's advice and the fact that they were now to be forced to spend the next few days in each other's company, she nevertheless quickly rejected the pattern prescribed by his mother. Exhortations to apply himself to his books, interspersed with trips to the coal shed, were not very likely to stimulate the forthcoming side of his nature and, by an extraordinary stroke of luck, the very first alternative that occurred to her landed plum on the bull's-eye

42

Adrian, it transpired, cherished a secret dream of learning to drive.

Everything was in his favour. Martha had time on her hands for once and her ramshackle old car, which had to struggle to achieve forty miles an hour, was due for the scrap heap in any case, long past the stage where a little more gear grinding or bumper bashing could affect its fate. Adrian had passed his seventeenth birthday and so was eligible for a provisional licence. Martha sent him down to the post office to pick up an application form and then telephoned Miranda to ask if she had kept her L plates.

'Matter of fact, I did, Martha. I felt like chucking them over a cliff as soon as I'd passed the bleeding test, but I'm too bloody mean. Why do you want to know?'

'I wondered if I might borrow them for a few days? The boy who's staying with me wants to practise with my car.'

'Okay, I'll dig them out for you, nothing easier. 'Fraid I can't bring them over, though. My Dad's taken the car to Lewes.'

'Never mind about that, we'll pick them up on our first outing. Will half an hour be too soon?'

'No, fine. Okay, Martha, see you!'

Adrian, as it turned out, was a natural. They sat in the car, inside the wooden shed which served as Martha's garage, while she laboriously instructed him in the theory of driving, her enthusiasm and confidence draining away as she saw how bored and impatient he was growing. But when he changed places with her and moved into the driving seat she found that none of it had been wasted. He was able to repeat everything she had told him and to slide in and

43

out of gear as though he had been doing it all his life.

'I believe you've been driving all your life,' she said accusingly.

'No, I haven't.'

'Well, if this is really your first go, Adrian, you'll be ready for Le Mans by this time next year.'

'Actually, my father did give me a few lessons last holidays, but my stepfather found out and he got my mother to stop it.'

'Oh, why was that?'

'Because that's the way he is. He pretended it was because I was under age, but that was just an excuse. We weren't going on the road or anything; just round the tracks on the estate, which doesn't count.'

'So what do you believe was his real objection?'

'Oh, I don't know. He probably told my mother I'd run over one of the workers or something and it would land him in a lot of trouble, even if it wasn't my fault. Awfully silly, but my father said it might make things difficult if we went on with it, so that was the end of that.'

'Too bad! But in view of what you've told me, do you think perhaps we should give up the idea? I know you're now legally entitled to be a Learner driver, but I wouldn't want to go against your parents' wishes. If they're likely to object, perhaps we should call it off?'

'It's not my parents,' he replied, throwing himself about in uncontrolled fury. 'Only my stepfather, don't you understand? He's not my legal guardian and I shan't be driving over his lousy property, so if he doesn't like it he can stuff it.'

This was a new Adrian with a vengeance and, although Martha had not been irresistibly attracted to the old one, she did not consider this to be a great improvement.

44

However, he had not entirely fallen from grace and after a moment muttered sheepishly, 'Sorry, Aunt Martha, I didn't mean to go on like that, but it's so jolly unfair. Whatever I want to do, he makes some excuse why I can't.'

'And you promise me it's just your stepfather? Not . . . the others who object to your driving?'

'Absolutely,' he replied firmly. 'Mum would be perfectly okay about it, if it weren't for Derek, and Dad too. It was his idea to teach me, in the first place.'

'Right!' she said, making up her mind to believe him. 'So now you can practise backing out. Only as far as the gate, mind! Then I'll take over until we get the L plates. Don't forget to release the handbrake and look in your rear mirror. There's not likely to be anything behind you, but it's important to get into the right routine from the start.

'Very good, indeed! Excellent!' she added, when he had completed this small exercise to perfection. 'It doesn't look as though the test will hold any terrors for you.'

He did not take his eyes away from the rear mirror, but he flushed with pride and pleasure and his mouth twitched into the beginnings of a smile. For the first time, she was aware of some glimmerings of latent charm.

Billy's car was blocking the entrance to his garage, so Martha parked hers in the lane.

'I'll wait here,' Adrian said, as she climbed out.

'Please yourself. I won't be long.'

Unaccustomed to being told to please himself, it left him high and dry, with nothing to sulk about. Possessing few other resources with which to while away the minutes, he soon got out of the car and went in search of her.

45

There were three people in the garage. One was Aunt Martha, looking worried sick as usual, another was an ugly looking bloke wearing whacking great glasses and leaning back against the wall with his arms folded and his eyes shut. The third was a girl of about his own age, or a bit older, who was standing in the middle of a great pile of junk, which included a lawn mower, some mouldy looking tennis racquets and a collection of battered paint tins. She was wearing a black leotard and a pair of much darned black tights, both of which were rather dusty. There was dust on her hair too and a greasy black streak down her face. Altogether, she looked a mess, but he had to admit, with a passing twinge of guilt, that she had pretty good proportions and the most stunning legs of any girl he had ever seen.

She was also in a foul temper.

'Damn it all, Martha, I know they were here,' she was saying, as she hurled bits of rubbish about in an ineffectual fashion. 'I'm absolutely certain of it. It was the obvious place to put them. Why the hell did someone have to go and move them?'

'Never mind, Miranda dear, it doesn't matter a bit. We can easily pass by Lubbock's and get another pair.'

'I know that; it's just that it annoys me to death not to be able to find something when I put it there myself.'

Nobody took the faintest notice of Adrian hovering on the sidelines, so he cleared his throat, inaudibly at first and then more noisily than he had intended. The girl glared at him briefly and the man opened his eyes and smiled with half his mouth, just as though he were too lazy to use the whole of it.

'May I know what you are looking for, my dearest?' he then asked, before shutting his eyes again.

'Those damned L plates. You haven't seen them, I suppose?'

'Not lately. Touch wood and all that, but it's some time since I had to change a wheel.'

'What's that got to do with it? I'm talking about L plates.'

'I heard you. They're in the boot, under that bit of sacking with the spare wheel.'

'What the hell are they doing there?'

'Well, it's where you put them, you know. I remember your saying it was the obvious place and, for once, I agreed with you.'

'Oh, hell and death!' Miranda said in a voice of doom. 'Are you now telling me that I've struggled to pull all this lot out and you had them in the boot all the time?'

'Yes, I am, and I should be most grateful if you would now struggle to put it all back again. I've no desire to leave my car out in the rain for the next six months.'

'Oh, all right, all right; don't go on about it. I'll see to it.'

Adrian nerved himself to clear his throat again.

'I'll give you a hand, if you like,' he croaked. 'I mean, some of that stuff looks a bit heavy.'

'Come along, Martha,' Billy said, taking her arm. 'You and I will go and sit down with a glass of sherry, as befits our age and station.'

'It's amazing, you know,' she remarked, as they strolled through the garden towards his studio, 'what wonders a little self-confidence can do for people, 'specially the very young.'

'Is it now?'

'Well, you know, Billy, Adrian's been staying with me for almost a week now and not once has he offered to help; not even to make his own bed. And yet ten minutes in the driving seat and a little well deserved praise and look at him now! Weighing in like a proper little gent!'

'Oh, Martha, what a wonderful woman you are!' Billy said, giving her arm a gentle squeeze. He was so amused that after a moment he had to remove his hand to take off his glasses and wipe the tears from his eyes.

< 3 >

'All the same,' Martha said at the end of two hours of three-point turns and stopping and starting on hills, 'we'll have to give it a rest tomorrow. Your stepfather is coming to lunch.'

'Oh, death and hell! Can't we have an hour's practice before that?'

'No, we can't. I'm sorry, Adrian, but you'll just have to be patient. I must go out early and get something to eat and Mrs Bailey doesn't come on Saturdays, so I'll have to cook it as well. Besides, I must somehow try and drop in and see your grandmother for ten minutes.'

'I'll go instead, if you'll give me half an hour in the evening.'

'But how could you possibly get there? You know very well that the hospital is four miles away.'

'Yes, but I was thinking. You're supposed to drive Derek back to the hotel after lunch, aren't you? What about dropping me off at the hospital on your way, and then collecting me coming back? You pass it, anyway.'

'You've got it all worked out, haven't you? Not for nothing, it seems, are you Christine's son. All right, it's a deal, but only on one condition. You've got to promise to find a way to tell your parents what you're up to. I see no reason why they should object, but I hate going behind people's backs and they may think it would be better for you to have lessons from a professional.'

'Oh no, they won't. My stepfather would never cough up for anything like that.'

Martha was about to point out that in this instance the onus would hardly lie with Derek, but then had to admit to herself that for all she knew Christine's curious design for living might apply as much to the economics of their joint household as to everything else and, furthermore, whether it did or not, Adrian could be forgiven for having become a little confused on the subject. Reverting instead to the main argument, she said, 'Nevertheless, I think it would be wrong to make any secret about it. The sooner it's out in the open, the better. Don't you agree?'

'No,' he said savagely, 'I don't. I think it's a lousy idea. I'm not a kid.'

'Then stop behaving like one and try to be sensible. This has nothing to do with your age. Well, let's leave it for the moment. We're both tired, I dare say. Come along indoors and we'll make ourselves a cup of tea. You can think it over and I'm sure you'll find I'm right.'

He did not answer, but stared fixedly at the dashboard and, suspecting that he was battling with tears, she said no more and left him to recover in his own time. It took him several minutes to do so and the kettle had already boiled by the time he came into the kitchen.

'Well, thanks for the lesson, anyway,' he mumbled, slumping down over the table, as she pottered about setting out mugs and biscuits, 'but you don't really understand.'

'Don't I?'

'No one does, not even Mum. She used to be fairly on the ball, but she keeps telling me how lucky I am.'

'In what way?'

'Oh, you know, having the three of them together and

all that. So that I've got two fathers taking an interest, instead of just one. Big deal!' he added with lugubrious irony.

'Well, perhaps you do score, in that sense?'

'Are you joking? It's absolute bloody hell. Most people of my age have just two parents interfering and laying down the law and nagging the whole time. Or only one, if they're lucky. I've got three of them at it and you know something, Aunt Martha? My life just damn well isn't worth living.'

SATURDAY, 11th AUGUST [DAYTIME]

Extract from Dolly Kershaw's letter to Alice Barnby:

. . . my girl could do such a thing to her own mother. It passes belief, and after leading me on, the way she has! Oh, you may count yourself lucky, dear, that you never had any children. And yet Christine used to be such a lovely little girl, when she was tiny. So sweet and obedient and such a beauty! How she's changed, though! I've thought for some time that she was growing hard, though I haven't liked to say so openly, even to you. I expect you've read between the lines, but I doubt if even you would have believed it could come to this. That I'm to be thrown on to the scrap heap, after all their promises! Because that's what going back to that sour-faced Martha amounts to, however much he may talk about things being more comfortable there in the future, whatever that's supposed to mean. And he's at the bottom of it. In my heart of hearts, I know that. My Christine would never be so cruel, however much she may have changed. And if she has it's him that's done it, you can be sure of that.

Of course he had the cheek to say it was mainly her decision and all the rest of it, and that it didn't do for the different generations to share a house (you notice that I'm supposed to share with Martha!) but he's got

51

round her in some way, because he's jealous, I see that now. If it was her idea, I said to him, why didn't she come and tell me so herself? That flummoxed him. He went as red as a beetroot, great fat booby that he is, and blurted out something about her being so sensitive and not wanting to hurt my feelings. But I could tell he was lying and how I despise him for it. If he was half a man he'd come straight out with it and not try to put the blame on her.

Well, dear, I feel a bit better now, after pouring out my troubles to you, but it's a wonder I'm here to tell the tale. Dr Mead says I've made a splendid recovery, but I've got to look out for myself and take things quietly, otherwise I could easily have another attack. Mr High and Mighty Marsh didn't think of that, did he? Fine fool he'd have looked sitting there and me having heart failure in front of his eyes! But I don't intend to give him that satisfaction. I refuse to upset myself over it. She's supposed to be coming to see me tomorrow (if he lets her) and I'm just going to lie here in my nice, comfy bed and work out my plans very carefully and calmly . . .

< 2 >

'Hope the poor kid gets a better reception than I did,' Derek said, as they drove away from the hospital. 'I dropped in there on my way over this morning, but I can't say the visit was an unqualified success.'

'Oh dear!' Martha said in genuine distress. 'I am sorry to hear that. She's been so much better lately, but, poor Dolly, it doesn't take much to upset her.'

'No, I can imagine, and I'm sorry I had to be the

one to do it, but the time had come to clear up a few misunderstandings and it was no good expecting Christine to take it on. She's too soft hearted. Well, thanks for the lunch, Martha. It was excellent and I ate far too much.'

She did not dispute this, considering it likely, moreover, that he made a regular habit of over-eating. He was such a huge, unwieldy man that it had been necessary to push the passenger seat as far back as it would go to fit him in at all. Even so, his legs were twisted at an awkward angle and, despite the off-loading of Adrian, who had been doubled up in the back seat, the car still seemed full to bursting point.

'I'm afraid we all impose on you, don't we?' he went on when Martha made no reply, 'but it wasn't my idea, you know. I wanted to take you both out to lunch somewhere, make a real treat of it, but Christine said it would do me good to have a bit of home cooking, for once, and I must say she was right, although it can't have been much of a change for you.'

'It was, in a way,' she admitted. 'Quite a nice change, you know, to cook for a man once in a while.'

'It was damn good,' he said. 'Must have set you back a packet, too. And speaking of that, Martha, there are one or two financial ends I'd like to tie up with you, now that we're on our own.'

Much to her embarrassment, he enlarged on these financial ends for several minutes, but she did not interrupt or try to change the subject, sensing that it was the one area in which he felt at home and in control. Also she had to pay extra attention to her driving because her movements were restricted, to some extent, by his sheer bulk and, in spite of all her care, she felt his full weight lurch against her as she made the left-hand turn into the grounds of the hotel. Glancing sideways in alarm, she saw that his face had become even more suffused and that he was breathing like a hippopotamus, as his hand struggled to reach down into his trouser pocket. The next minute a tiny square parcel landed in her lap.

'There you are, my dear. Came across that when I was in London and thought it might suit you. If you don't like it, wrap it up again and send it to someone for Christmas.'

'I can't open it now,' she said, smiling.

'No, that wasn't the idea. Wait till you get home.'

'Well, it's extremely kind of you, Derek. I'm sure it's something lovely and I'll thank you properly when I've seen what it is.'

'No,' he said, with self-conscious gruffness, 'no need for that. Rather you didn't, in fact. I enjoy spending money on silly trinkets. About all the fun I do get nowadays. So no thanks, if you don't mind, Martha.'

'Very well, I'll have to restrain myself, if that's what you want. Were you able to fix up everything with Billy, by the way?'

'Oh yes, no problems. None that can't be ironed out, anyway. Chris thought he was a bit woolly and that all the estimates were far too high, but then she's out of touch, you know. Besides, I don't believe in skimping, do you?'

'Not when it can be avoided, no. Anyway, I'm glad everything's been settled.'

'Yes, I think your Billy Jones has got his head screwed on all right, despite appearances. I took him for the sissy type at first, but then I'm out of touch too and I appear to be wrong. No, the only thing that remains to be done now is choosing the wallpaper and so on. I'm meeting him at the house tomorrow morning, so that we can look at some patterns on the spot. Have to get Christine along for that. She's a wizard at it; marvellous sense of colour. Well, cheers, Martha! And thanks again.'

'Can you manage to get out, or shall I come round and open the door?'

'I'll manage,' he said and, after some prolonged heaving and pushing, was as good as his word.

Martha placed the little parcel in the glove compartment, then waved goodbye and drove off towards the hospital.

Only twenty minutes had elapsed since dropping him off there and she was distinctly annoyed to see Adrian seated on the low wall which enclosed the car park of the private wing, literally kicking his heels against the brickwork.

'Not my fault,' he said, in answer to her reproachful look. 'She's not there.'

'What do you mean, Adrian? What have they done with her now?'

'She beat it. Went off by herself.'

'What are you talking about, my dear? They would never have discharged her without warning me.'

'No, they haven't. She hasn't gone for good. The nurse told me Grandmother had asked the doctor if it would be all right for her to go for a drive this afternoon and he said it would, so she rang up the taxi place and they collected her at three o'clock. She said she'd only be gone for about an hour. Can I take over the wheel now?'

'No, you can't,' she said crossly.

'Oh, why? You promised.'

'Well, that was before I knew this was going to happen.'

'I don't see what difference it makes,' he grumbled. 'I mean, just because Grandmother goes for a drive, I can't see why . . .'

'Then use your imagination. Hasn't it struck you that

the most likely place for her to have gone is home? And I haven't even washed up the lunch yet.'

He did not chip in at this point with offers of help, giving rise to the passing reflection that his reformation had been short-lived, but her main preoccupation was with her mental picture of what could now be taking place at the cottage. It was not so much the piles of dirty dishes which dismayed her as the disheartening recollection of having left a half-full bottle of wine, not to mention the sherry decanter, in full view on the sideboard. The moment they reached the house she bolted inside, leaving Adrian to get over his disappointment at his own sluggish pace, and made straight for the dining room.

Everything was exactly as she had left it, and it was the same story in each of the other rooms, both upstairs and down. Whatever had inspired Dolly to undertake her mysterious outing, it was clearly not from any desire to visit her own home. Pondering on the various alternatives and debating as to whether she should make some tactful enquiries at the local off-licence, Martha mechanically took down her apron from behind the scullery door and began stacking the first load of dirty silver and glasses on to a tray.

However, before she was even half-way through the washing and drying up, another and even more disagreeable idea flitted into her head and, without even stopping to remove her apron, she began to hunt for the car keys. Only when they had failed to materialise in any of the usual places did it occur to her that she might have left them in the ignition. Blind panic having by then given way to chronic anxiety, she called out to Adrian, who had slunk upstairs to Dolly's room, which he was now occupying, that she would be going out for ten minutes, then returned to the car and set off in the direction of Bookers Farm.

* * *

There was a sharp left-hand turn off the road and down a narrow, rutted lane, which led to the farm entrance. As Martha approached it, a car, which she recognised as one of Lubbock's, nosed out and turned left into the road. The driver, in his peaked cap, was nearest to her, but she was fairly certain that there was a woman passenger in the back seat. Dolly always rode in the back, considering it to be more suited to her dignity.

Martha automatically continued towards her destination, though wondering now if there was any purpose in it. The evidence suggested that Dolly was safe and sound and on her way back to the hospital and, in retrospect, she could see that it had been a foolish impulse which had brought her out, in the first place. Everyone in the neighbourhood was well aware of the cause of Mrs Kershaw's accident and it was highly improbable that Lubbock or one of his drivers would have sat meekly by and allowed her to wander into the house unaccompanied.

The obvious course was to turn round and go home again, but the thought of the chores which awaited her there was not inviting and it was such a glorious late summer afternoon that, with her mind now at rest and soothed still further by the gentle, curving countryside around her, she fell to the temptation to play truant for just a little longer. She parked the car in the midden, which had now been transformed into a builder's yard, with piles of rubble, a cement mixer and old and new pipes strewn all over it, then climbed over a fence which separated it from a meadow and began to walk.

At first, the only sounds came from the birds and the steady champing of some Friesian cows, who glanced up haughtily as she passed, but, wandering in a diagonal direction over the upward curve of the field, these were blotted out by a continuous mechanical hum and, on reaching the crest, she saw Robert Meyer's enormous new red combine harvester slashing through the barley in the field below.

It reminded her of the existence of other human beings and of the strange figure she must cut, a thin, gawky creature, still wearing her ridiculous flowered apron, meandering through the fields on her own. She turned quickly back to the car, but having reached it found herself gripped by yet another compulsion. She walked over to the new wing on the west side of the farmhouse, passed through a pink door frame and embarked on a slow and exhaustive tour of the premises.

Back home again at last, she telephoned the hospital and was told that the patient had returned. She was a little tired, but in good spirits, and the outing was believed to have done her good.

SATURDAY, 11th AUGUST [EVENING]

'The only faint consolation,' Martha said after dinner, 'is that since he particularly asked me not to thank him, he probably wouldn't wish me to wear it in his presence either. That's one thing I certainly can't do, and the other is to claim the insurance, because I have no idea what it was or how much it was worth.'

She was spending the evening with Avril, who was determined to use every hour of Dolly's absence to the best advantage, and Billy was also present, although this was mainly on account of the fact that Robert Meyer, Avril's husband, was away on a fishing trip in Scotland. Although the kindest of men, there was something formidably self-assured and authoritative in Robert's manner, which so unnerved Billy that he could not often be enticed into the house when the master was at home. Adrian and Miranda had also been included in the invitations, but had been shooed away to the billiard room as soon as dinner was over. It was only then that Martha had broached the subject of Derek's present.

'If you know so little about it, how can you tell it was worth insuring?' Billy enquired without much interest.

'Well, now you mention it,' Martha replied, turning her anxious gaze on him, 'how do I? The shape, perhaps? It looked like a jeweller's box. But there must have been something else, surely? Oh yes, I remember now, he said something about enjoying spending money on trinkets. I suppose that gave me the idea it might be a brooch, or something of that kind.'

'Now, let's try and be practical for a moment,' said Avril, who was virtually incapable of being anything else. 'How long was it left unguarded in the car altogether?'

'From about half past three, when Adrian and I got home, until I was changing to come here. I remembered it then and I thought I might as well wear it for you. When I went out to the car it had gone. Perhaps I dreamt the whole thing.'

'But, presumably, any passer-by could have walked in and pinched it while you were washing up? There's no door on your garage and I bet the car wasn't locked.'

'Good gracious, no. Not a day passes when I don't go out there in the hopes that it's been stolen. But I think that's rather far-fetched, Avril. I mean, to come snooping round on the off-chance that I'd just been given a small box, which might contain jewellery and which I might have left in the glove compartment! I can't quite see it.'

'Maybe so, but that's not altogether the point. When my jewellery was stolen a few years ago Robert and I had to answer the most idiotic questions you ever heard. It's known as covering every eventuality and you then proceed to eliminate the impossibles.'

'I agree with Martha that you can start with that one,' Billy said.

'Very well, we'll pass on to the next. How long was the car left unattended at Bookers while you went for your stroll? This is rather fun, isn't it? Perhaps I should have been a detective.'

'Oh, not more than half an hour,' Martha replied. 'And there was no one about. Apart from your harvesters, I didn't see a soul.'

'We can rule them out,' Avril said firmly, evidently not

inclined to waste her powers of detection on her own farm hands. 'How about the builders?'

'On Saturday afternoon?'

'Oh, it has been known, hasn't it, Billy? But still, I don't suppose they would have come on foot, whether for legitimate reasons, or otherwise. So what comes next?'

'If I were you, I'd stop beating my brains out over it,' Billy said impatiently. 'Why not just tell Marsh that you've lost his present and would like him to replace it?'

'Yes, you can see me doing that, can't you?'

'I can see him taking it in his stride. I never met a man more anxious to chuck his money about.'

Martha was so dumbfounded by this statement that she opened her mouth and stared in wonderment, all of which was lost on Billy, whose eyes were now shut. So she turned to Avril, saying thoughtfully, 'It's the most extraordinary thing, but Billy could be right, you know. He's certainly been most generous to me, hasn't he? I took that to be a special case; more of a conscience salver than anything else, but why should I have thought that? It's not his old mother, after all. The truth is, you know, that I've been brainwashed by Adrian. It was so unperceptive of me because anyone can see that the poor child has a positive phobia about his stepfather. Really, the more I think about it the more I see that Billy has got it right.'

'Of course he has,' Avril said. 'It's one of the reasons why he's been so moody ever since they all arrived here.'

'I don't follow you. I thought it was the skinflint clients who were so depressing?'

'Not this time. He'd been listening to all those tales about Christine's husband being such a disagreeable old Scrooge and he'd allowed himself to hope. Hadn't you, Billy?'

'Hope what?' Martha asked in deepest bewilderment.

'That the second marriage would end on the rocks, just like the first one, only this time he'd be around to pick up the pieces. Isn't that right, Billy?'

'You're a sentimental ass, Avril. All that was over twenty years ago.'

'Oh, was it? You don't fool me, old boy. I've seen you blushing and stammering like a sixteen-year-old every time her name was mentioned.'

'That happens to be a load of rubbish, and I would also remind you that I am now married to someone else.'

'What's that got to do with it? We all know that boring old Daphne caught you on the rebound.'

'Nevertheless, the bonds of rebound are just as binding as the other sort and we are still married.'

'And Christine is a good deal more married than you are, in a sense,' Martha pointed out. 'She seems delighted with the arrangement too. It's quite odd, but I dare say there are lots of women who would secretly enjoy having two husbands. She's one of the rare ones who have achieved it. I don't mean in a sex way,' she added hastily. 'With her it's more a question of craving for admiration, perhaps in larger doses than any one man could supply. And then, you see, once something belongs to her, she's never very ready to give it up. What puzzles me is the docile way these two men submit to it; sharing her, as it were.'

'It doesn't puzzle me at all,' Avril said. 'They're both fundamentally weak characters, who've allowed themselves to be jockeyed into the most ludicrous situation; one for the sake of peace and the other because he didn't want to lose his job. And, whatever you may say, your cousin is a proper little sex pot. Now that I've met her, I see it all clearly. She may bore the pants off you and me, but she's certainly got something for the gentlemen. She's a female spider and those two spineless flies couldn't break out of her web, however much they wanted to. If we're not careful, we shall find Billy getting invited into the parlour too. I'm sure Christine would hate to feel there was a man alive who wouldn't come running, if she beckoned.'

'You've overlooked one vital factor,' Billy told her. 'I may be a spineless fly, but I'm not nearly grand enough for Christine now. The only thing I represent for her is a lucky escape.'

'All the same, I expect she'd have become more human, if you'd married her,' Martha said kindly. "Specially if you'd stood up to her a bit.'

'I don't believe I would have, you know. I never stood up to Daphne. The idea that one of you has to be the dominant partner always strikes me as rather vulgar. And Derek's way round the problem appeals to me even less.'

'What is it?' Avril asked, sitting forward in her chair.

'Too devious to be believed. He made it quite clear that Christine is for ever badgering him to get everything done on the cheap and finally he came to the point and asked me to put in two separate accounts for the fittings and fixtures. One is to give the prices as Christine would like them to be, and the other as they are. She is shown the first one and he gives me a cheque for the second. It is really too childish for words.'

Avril said, 'It is just the kind of thing I would expect. Weak people will always fight like dogs to avoid a showdown. What really fascinates me is the part that Tim Whitfield plays in this particular charade. Is he in Derek's confidence, or just as much fooled as the lady?'

'Perhaps he doesn't care. It's not his money, after all; or his wife, come to that.'

The discussion had moved on to a level where Martha felt slightly uncomfortable. It was not only the sense of

63

disloyalty she experienced in sitting passively by and hearing her cousin's character so coolly dissected which worried her. There was also the fear that Adrian, who made rather a practice of furtive loitering, might even now have his ear pinned to the keyhole. She stood up, saying, 'If you don't mind, Avril, I think it's time I took my charge home.'

Billy yawned. 'And high time my charge took me home. I've got a meeting with the client on the site at eleven tomorrow, so no day of rest this Sunday.'

'It's only ten,' Avril protested, 'and the charges seem to be getting along splendidly. Can't we give them a few more minutes?'

'You forget, my dear, that we still have to go through the scene where Adrian wants to drive home, so that he can get some practice in the dark. He says he will and I say he won't and the argument goes on for at least ten minutes.'

'Oh, fiddle-de-dee,' Avril said, getting up with a bound. 'We'll see about that! You stay here and I'll soon tell Master Adrian where he gets off.'

In less than three minutes she was back.

'Prepare yourselves,' she warned. 'The charges have flown.'

'Oh, in that case,' Billy announced indifferently, 'I shall go home without mine. How about you, Martha?'

'You'll have to get Martha to drive you. They've taken your car.'

'Oh no,' Martha wailed, literally wringing her hands, which always suffered from a loss of circulation when she became nervous or worried. 'Oh, they can't have, Avril. Where could they have gone at this time of night?'

'Hold on to your seat, my dear, because there's worse to come. Billy's car has gone and so have the L plates

64

from yours. I think we may safely assume that Adrian is getting some practice in the dark,' she added, with great amusement, which Martha could neither share nor see the reason for.

'Oh dear, oh dear, how very dreadful of him! And how naughty of Miranda to encourage him! He's quite inexperienced, you know.'

'Don't get the wind up, Martha, they'll be perfectly safe, I feel sure. If I know anything, they'll keep well clear of the main roads and they won't necessarily be doing much driving either. If you want to go home, why not drop Billy off and I'll deliver Adrian to you later?'

'Oh, no thank you, Avril. You're very kind, but I know I could never sleep a wink until he was safe at home. I feel so responsible. I'd rather wait here for them, if you don't mind.'

'Then for goodness sake, have a proper drink, instead of that poisonous lemon stuff.'

'I ought not to. You know how silly and indiscreet I become after only one drink.'

'Do I? I wonder. Sometimes it seems to me that small doses of alcohol just give you the courage to say what you've been wanting to say all along.'

'That's exactly what I mean,' Martha explained patiently, nevertheless accepting the whisky and soda which Avril handed her. 'However, as everything seems to be slipping out of control, I suppose I may as well swim with the tide and go downhill myself. I've been thinking, you know,' she added after a pause for refreshment. 'When I first met Adrian he reminded me in some ways of his mother, but I see now that it's worse than that. What I've really got on my hands is another little embryo Dolly.'

SUNDAY, 12th AUGUST

On Sunday morning, when Billy was beginning some half-hearted preparations for his appointment at Bookers Farm, Christine telephoned to ask if he would mind postponing it for an hour or so.

'We forgot about the church services starting so late,' she explained.

'Don't tell me you're going to church, Christine?'

'Not me, but Derek and Tim want to. I know you're all heathens and atheists over here, but things are different where we come from.'

'So why aren't you going yourself?'

'I'll probably drop in and see Mother for half an hour, which is a far more Christian act, in its way. They can pick me up afterwards and we'll all come on to Bookers together.'

'What time do you want to make it, then?'

Her voice faded, as she turned to speak to someone in the room with her, not bothering to cover the mouthpiece, so that he could hear male voices in the background and even a burst of laughter, as he waited, half dressed and shuddering with cold and impatience. She came back in full voice, saying, 'They want to know if twelve-thirty would be too late for you?'

'Yes, I'm afraid it would. We lunch at one and Miranda is a great little tartar.'

'Oh, Billy darling, couldn't you ask her to make it

half an hour later, just for once? I'm dying to get all this settled, so that the work can go ahead, but we have so many things to pack in.'

'I dare say you have, but cooking the Sunday joint is not one of them.'

'Goodness, what a bully you've become. Oh, sorry, hang on a minute, Derek's saying something.'

Once more he waited, twisting and tugging at his dressing-gown cord and mouthing to himself in a frenzy of annoyance. Then Derek's voice, sounding disgustingly jocular in the circumstances, took over.

'Sorry about all that, old chap, but I'd really like to go to church and Tim certainly ought to, since it seems to be his saint's day. Would twelve-fifteen suit you?'

'Very well, if that's the best you can do.'

Christine came floating back with the regulation tea-spoonful of sugar to sweeten the pill.

'You are an angel, Billy. I know we must be a frightful nuisance to you, but we do appreciate everything you're doing, and giving up your Sunday morning and everything. Truly! I'll do something terribly nice for you in return one day, I promise.'

'Just try very hard not to be late, for once, Christine. That's all I want from you.'

'All right, darling. See you later. Goodbye.'

< 2 >

Half a mile away, in an upstairs room in Martha's cottage, Adrian was hunched over his letter to Diana. It was a tough one, too. He had not added a single line to the half page which had been lying hidden among his underpants ever since Aunt Martha had stammered out her diffident,

67

momentous offer to teach him to drive. His whole life had changed from that moment on, which should have made it a lot easier to dig up things to say to Di, but he was finding, to his disgust and despair, that it was not only much harder, but that for the first time since leaving Africa he was strongly disinclined to make the effort.

One of the main obstacles was his strange inability to capture a mental picture of her face. Every time he attempted it the vision of a girl in a black leotard, dancing in the moonlight to an audience consisting only of himself and one black and white cow, swam into the foreground, blotting out Diana's elusive features.

As a last resort, he forced himself to re-read her latest letter, which was quite a chore, because she wasn't much good at describing things and also her lavish endearments made him feel more guilty than ever. However, it enabled him to fill up another page by telling her that he was glad her pony had been so pleased to see her back for the holidays, that the Warrens' picnic sounded like fun and he was sorry to have missed it; and, having in this way achieved quite a respectable length, he came to the two paragraphs which he had been saving for the end and which, as well as being the easiest to write, were intended to compensate for the inadequacy of all the rest.

I haven't forgotten your birthday, by the way, and I hope this arrives in time to say Many Happies. I've already got your present, but will have to keep it till we meet. For one thing, if I post it, it will have to be registered (!!!) which might lead to complications at your end. So I've put it in a VERY SAFE PLACE. You'd never guess in a million years!!!

It seemed rather inartistic to follow this sensational

item with a reference to his own affairs, so he put it in a postscript:

PS. Almost forgot to tell you that I've applied for the driving test. Won't it be bliss to throw away those bloody L plates?

< 3 >

Billy Jones had arrived at Bookers Farm at ten minutes past twelve in a mood of deep pessimism, which was temporarily dispelled by the pleasant surprise of finding a black saloon car already parked in the midden. Tim was the only occupant and when Billy drew up alongside he leant out of the driver's window and gave him one of his wide grins, accompanied by a flamboyant military salute.

'Aren't you coming in?' Billy asked him.

'Not yet, old chap. We've split up for the present and I'm the blinking shover. Chris – wait for it! – wasn't quite ready. She wanted to go back to the hotel and brush the smell of hospital out of her hair, or something. Derek was getting the wind up about keeping you waiting, so we thought the best plan would be to deliver him and I'll go back for Madam. I'm just on my way to carry out mission number two. Shouldn't take more than half an hour.'

'If it does, I can't guarantee to be here when you return,' Billy said, closing his eyes. He was thinking that a simpler alternative to this complicated programme would have been to beat Christine over the head with her hairbrush and throw her into the car, but one could not

69

expect this kind of treatment to recommend itself to the men in her life.

'Is Derek inside?' he asked.

'Yes, just gone in. He thought there were probably one or two – er – you know, business matters, which you and he could sort of hammer out while you're waiting. Anyway, I'll get cracking. See you later.'

He saluted again, then backed out of the gate and shot off down the lane.

Billy returned to his own car, gathered up the books of wallpaper patterns from the back seat and staggered up to the house with them, pushing his load against the front door like a battering ram. It was unlatched and swung open into the central hall, where a wall separating it from the old kitchen had been knocked down to make one imposing rectangular room, with a new wide polished wooden staircase going up through the middle of it.

Beside the foot of the staircase there was a wooden plank, supported on two three-cornered stools, and Billy pushed aside a carpenter's saw, which was lying on top of it, to make a space for the books. Having shed his load, he remained leaning over the top of it, panting from exhaustion. They turned to pants of apoplexy when he saw, to his fury, that the telephone had been disconnected.

It was an old-fashioned, cumbersome instrument, which had been the subject of a running battle between himself and the telephone company, who were proposing to cut it off. Billy was equally determined that they should not and the argument had finally been settled, in the simplest possible manner, by Avril sending a cheque for the surprisingly large account which the former tenant had left unpaid. Even allowing for the inevitable delays of bureaucracy, the money should have reached the right department over a week ago and he had allowed himself to believe that the

danger was passed. Moreover, there was something vaguely disquieting in the sight of the truncated wires sticking
out of the wainscoting, which was quite distinct from the
inconvenience it betokened for himself and the prospective
owners, but before he could pin it down his eye was caught
by a new excrescence. This was a pile of wood blocks on
the other side of the room and, even from a distance of
twenty feet, he could see that, instead of the teak he had
ordered, these were made of some inferior imitation, with
which the miserable Cafferty or his henchmen had no
doubt been hoping to put across a fast one.

He walked over to the pile and gave it a sharp kick,
to show his contempt for such amateurish chicanery, then
stood staring down into the newly exposed ingle fireplace,
with its ancient and beautifully preserved bread oven, almost disappointed in his irritation not to be able to find
any fault with the bricks which had been used for matching
up the broken sections.

All in all, about ten minutes had gone by before he remembered that he was supposed to be hatching financial
plots with Derek Marsh and embarked on a search of the
premises, which he was subsequently to describe on several
occasions as follows:

Going first to the new wing and finding no one
in the kitchen or other downstairs rooms, he returned
to the hall and stood at the bottom of the stairs calling
Marsh's name. Getting no answer, he plodded upstairs
and into the principal bedroom, which was filled with
radiators and copper pipes, then on to the second bedroom, where the plasterers had been at work, peeling
off layers of emulsion paint and dingy wallpaper, and
so on all through the upper storey, both new and old,
without encountering anyone at all.

When he had traversed both passages, which branched

71

out from each side of the central stairwell, he saw that the improvised door at the far end of the second one, shutting off the old ladder staircase, which was due to be demolished, had been left partly open, and he lashed out with another kick and closed it. The physical outburst did something to relieve his feelings and, resigning himself to a search through the outhouses, he started off downstairs again.

Even as he went, a kind of uneasiness connected with the open door overcame him and, although he tried to ignore it, and continue at the same pace, it needed only the sight of the saw, still balancing on the plank below, to transform the vague, amorphous fear into a tight ball of feverish anxiety. Pivoting round, he tore upstairs again, raced along the passage and pulled open the temporary door.

It could well have been the last act of his life, because the change from brilliant to dimmest of lights momentarily blinded him and, when he put out a tentative, fumbling foot for the top stair, it made no contact. Only the fact that he had instinctively been half prepared for this enabled him to draw back in time and save himself from falling from top to bottom of the steep and rickety staircase as surely as he now felt convinced Derek Marsh had done.

There was a light switch on the wall beside him, but the electricity was cut off at the main during weekends and he was far too shortsighted to identify a single object in the depths below. The staircase led straight down into the old combined scullery and bathroom, which was scheduled for conversion into a streamlined cloakroom and utility room, and so any of the vague shapes he could distinguish from above could have been pieces of equipment, covered with sacking.

72

There was nothing for it, therefore, but to return by the way he had come, down the new staircase, through the hall, where he briefly eyed the telephone in passing, and on to the scullery. As he entered it the last faint doubt was removed, for Derek was lying in a huge, sprawling, untidy heap just inside the door at the foot of the staircase and Billy knew for certain that he was dead.

For form's sake, he lifted one of the great cold hands, but even while he felt for a non-existent pulse, automatically staring at his watch and, as he realised later, registering the time as eighteen minutes past twelve, three-quarters of his mind was already occupied in planning his next move.

He really had small choice, for the nearest telephone was over a mile away and this was hardly an event which could be explained in a note pinned to the front door, to be read during his absence. So after a few minutes he got up off his knees and went out to the midden, to draw some fresh air into his lungs, and then returned to his car to await the arrival of the widow and her one remaining husband.

MONDAY, 13th AUGUST

'Tell me something, Avril; do you recall ever having had your telephone cut off?'

'No, I can't say I do. Robert is so strict and methodical, you know. Why do you ask?'

'Because it has happened to me several times.'

'How annoying for you! Or wasn't it?'

'Not particularly, although I can't pretend there weren't certain disadvantages. The trouble was that Daphne would keep hiding the bills.'

'Whatever for?'

'You may well ask, but she pretended it was because she was frightened to show them to me. She spent half her life on the telephone, as you know, so naturally the bills were enormous. Not that I really minded. So long as she was using the thing it at least meant that no one could get through to me. Daphne understood that, of course, but she always had to turn everything into a three-act drama, even when she was the one to lose most by it.'

'Well, this is a jolly little tiptoe back into the past, but what is it leading to?'

'Just that, being so familiar with the procedure, I am rather worried by what happened to the telephone at Bookers Farm, particularly as you'd already paid the bill by then.'

'And asked for a receipt, which they'd sent me; but

74

it doesn't necessarily follow that they'd have relayed the news to their engineering department.'

'I think they probably would have, but the point is, Avril, that I have this faculty for storing up useless information and I know that when you're cut off it's all done in some mysterious way at the exchange. The idea is that when you've been sufficiently humbled you can pay a small charge and be reconnected at a moment's notice. In all my vast experience, I never once remember an engineer coming to the house to cut through the wires, as happened at Bookers.'

'Yes, I see what you mean, Billy, it does seem strange. What about Cafferty's morons, though? Couldn't one of them have done it by mistake?'

'Not on your life. One of the main reasons why we fought to keep the line open was so that Cafferty could be in touch with his office. And the men were always telephoning their wives to say they'd be late home and all the rest of it. It was their only contact with the outside world and they were just as keen not to lose it as I was.'

Avril regarded him thoughtfully. 'Yes, I think I follow your drift, but there must be some less drastic explanation. What about vandals, for instance?'

'I'm afraid they have to be ruled out, too. It's true that anyone could have got in. There wasn't even the need to smash a window because the new wing is open to the winds; but, on the other hand, it's a long way to go to do such a tame bit of damage as that and nothing else has been touched. Without letting on what was in my mind, I asked Cafferty if he thought it was safe to leave all those tools and materials lying around and he told me there'd never been any trouble, or anything missing.'

Avril sighed. 'Well, I can see you've given a lot of

75

thought to it, even if you haven't quite come up with the answer, so just tell me this, old boy: how much difference did it actually make?'

Billy closed his eyes before answering. 'Not a lot, but enough, I expect. Christine and Tim didn't turn up until almost a quarter to one, so that was half an hour wasted. And I couldn't very well break the news in a couple of terse sentences, could I?'

'Not very well, no.'

'So that took up at least another five minutes. At the end of which, as you may already know, Christine launched into hysterics.'

'Yes, Martha tells me she was still having them yesterday evening.'

'She kept moaning on about how someone in Africa must have followed them over here, in order to murder Derek. Complete bunkum, of course.'

'But interesting, don't you think, Billy, that she immediately assumed it wasn't an accident?'

'In a way, but you can't attach too much importance to it. She was also threatening to sue the builders for criminal negligence and, for good measure, she threw in a bit about how depressed Derek had been at the prospect of settling in England and how worried about money, if you please! Altogether, the ground was pretty thoroughly covered for suicide, murder and accident.'

'And what was Tim doing during this tirade?'

'Same as me; trying to calm her down and being just about as ineffectual. There wasn't much to choose between us.'

'All of which added considerably to the delay, presumably?'

'Exactly. We managed to quieten her in the end, and she didn't want to view the remains, or anything like that.

76

It was agreed that Tim should take her back to the hotel and I would do what was necessary. As soon as they'd left, I bolted home to telephone. After that I went back to the Farm again and waited for the police and ambulance to arrive, which I must say they did in double quick time. Nevertheless, if the Bookers telephone had been in working order, they'd have been there at least an hour sooner and, if there had been any life left in him after that fall, it is an hour which could have been vital.'

'Whereas, if death had been instantaneous, it would have been easier to pinpoint the exact moment? It does begin to look rather sinister. Have you said anything about it to Martha?'

'Good heavens, no. Nor to anyone else and I beg you not to, either. Wouldn't it be implying that Tim had gone into the house with Marsh, before I arrived, had pushed him downstairs and then cut the telephone wires, for good measure?'

'But you don't mind implying that to me?'

'Because you're not remotely involved. And I'm such a coward that I have to share this burden with someone.'

'So you're not only implying it, you actually believe that's what did happen?'

'No,' he said slowly, 'I really don't, you know. Not Tim. Leaving aside the fact that he was my boyhood friend and all that, which you would rightly consider irrelevant, there are various factors in his favour. One is that I was on the early side for the appointment and I simply don't see how there could have been time for him to carry out such a programme. Apart from manoeuvring Marsh into the right position for the push which, no matter how carefully he'd worked out the method in advance, obviously couldn't have been done in a tremendous hurry. And that wouldn't have been the end of it. There still remained the telephone to deal with and all I can tell you is that, when I drove in, he was sitting in the car as good as gold, not the slightest bit ruffled or out of breath. What I find equally conclusive is that he didn't make any attempt to detain me. Quite the reverse, in fact. Now, if the purpose of cutting the telephone wires was to delay things, and I can see no other, wouldn't he have used every means in his power to keep me out there talking for as long as possible?'

'One would think so, I agree. How about the police reaction, though? Did they say "Tut tut, too bad!" or did you feel they suspected funny business?'

'No idea. I wasn't encouraged to linger and I wasn't keen to. I simply waited till they turned up, told them where to look for the deceased and then made off. They took my name and address, which they knew perfectly well already, and said they'd be round to my house later for a full statement.'

'And were they?'

'Within the hour. Old Tubby came in person and accepted a glass of port.'

'I'll bet. Did you tell him about the telephone?'

'Had to, didn't I, to explain why his men hadn't been notified sooner? But I tried to sound casual about it, as though it had no special significance and, as far as I know, it worked. He didn't hammer the point and, with any luck, that's the last I'll hear of it. It's up to them to delve a little deeper, if they want to, but they won't get any nudging from me.'

'Oh, I think that's a feeble attitude,' Avril said. 'You should try to be more public-spirited. The whole affair sounds distinctly fishy to me and I can't say I'm pleased about it. In my opinion, Derek gave every indication of being far and away the most superior member of that odd trio and, if someone did push him downstairs, I consider they deserve everything they get. Also it seems so rough on Martha. You mark my words, when Christine learns about that annuity, she'll scrub it with one stroke of the pen. Then bang goes the new car and all the other extras Martha thought she had coming to her.'

'All the same,' Billy pointed out, 'catching the criminal, if there is one, won't get any of it back for her. Personally, now that I've relieved my mind on the subject, I can see that I was most likely exaggerating the sinister elements and I hope that interest in the case dies down as soon as possible and the whole business is forgotten.'

'Well, as to that, my dear old ostrich, I think you've left something out of your calculations. There's bound to be an inquest and you'll be the star witness. You do realise that?'

'Only too well,' he replied gloomily. 'They've warned me already. It's on Wednesday.'

'And I doubt very much if the Coroner will let you off so lightly when he hears about the disconnected telephone. If I know anything, you'll be in for a grilling, my boy.'

TUESDAY, 14th AUGUST

Christine's hysteria continued unabated through Sunday night and most of Monday. It had tailed off, to some extent, by the evening, but had a brief revival on Tuesday, when a Mr Charles Lawson came down from London, at her request.

He was a cousin of some other Lawsons of Nairobi, whose firm had acted as solicitors to the Marsh family for two generations and, immediately on arriving in England, Derek had transferred his business to Charles. On Monday, Christine had telephoned him with the news of Derek's death and the following day he answered the summons in person. She spent an hour closeted with him in her private sitting room at the hotel and had emerged looking angry, as well as tearful. As soon as he had departed she burst into fresh storms of sobbing, but rallied sufficiently an hour or two later to pick up the telephone and ask for Martha's number.

'How are you, my dear?' Martha said, when she heard the tear-choked voice. 'Is there anything at all I can do?'

'Yes, there is. Oh God, it's so awful, how am I going to bear it?'

'Yes, Christine, I know, I know.'

'No, you don't, nobody does. It was bad enough before, but at least I believed that Adrian and I were secure. I didn't realise that I should practically have to earn a living scrubbing floors.'

'Oh, come now! I can't believe it's as desperate as all that.'

'Yes, it is; jolly nearly, anyway. Derek's been spending money like water ever since we came to England. Well, I don't have to tell you, of all people, do I? And now we're stuck with this house and everything.'

'If it's any comfort to you, Christine, that's one thing you can put your mind at rest over, right away. Avril won't mind in the least if you want to back out.'

'No, I dare say not, seeing she's already had the deposit.'

'She'll give it back, I promise you. She would never have breathed a word of this, but I know for a fact that since then she's had several offers for it, much higher than she let you have it for.'

'Is that so?' Christine asked, in such a comparatively calm and sensible tone that Martha, congratulating herself on having brought some immediate solace to the stricken widow, proceeded to lay it on even thicker.

'Yes, I assure you. Prices have gone up wildly in the last few months. She could probably get twice as much for it now, so you're in the clear on that score.'

'On the other hand, I suppose we shall still need a roof over our heads? Presumably no one expects us to be actually thrown on to the streets?'

'No, I'm sure they don't. If it comes to the pinch, I suppose we could always squeeze you in here for a day or two, while you get things straightened out.'

'Oh, that's kind of you, Martha! I knew I could rely on you and I would be most frantically grateful if you could keep Adrian for the time being. He'll be going to this crammer's place next month and the fees are astronomical. I simply can't afford hotel bills for him, as well.'

'Well, all right, Christine. I expect it can be managed, so long as your mother's in hospital.'

'Ah well, I was coming to that and I'm afraid I can't possibly justify keeping her there any longer. Anyway, they want her room. Matron told me so when I was there on Sunday. And Charles says I simply must find ways of cutting down as much as possible. He said that was one unnecessary expense I could very well do without.'

'Charles who?'

'Lawson. You know, I told you, he's Derek's solicitor. He's being frightfully kind and helpful and he thinks I may just be able to scrape along, if I cut down on inessentials and maybe find ways of making a little money here and there. You know, Martha, thinking of what you said about the house, it strikes me that it might be a good plan to divide it in half and let off one part. Not very nice to have other people living on top of one, but beggars can't be choosers and we don't really need more than three bedrooms now. I am sure Billy could tack on a little extra kitchen somewhere. I must speak to him about it.'

'Coming back to the present, Christine, are you saying that you wish me to have your mother back here and Adrian too?'

'Well, yes, if you could. I know it's not very convenient for you having to give up your dining room, but I've already explained that it will only be for a few weeks. Besides, you've got that tiny room in the attic which isn't being used. Why not put him in there?'

'It's full of trunks and all sorts of things. I haven't cleared it out for years.'

'Never mind, Adrian and I can help you with that. Not tomorrow, though. There's the inquest to get through and if my clothes don't arrive in time I shall have to dash out early and get myself something to wear for it.'

'Oh, really? Can't you make do with what you've got?'

'No, I can't. They're all terribly bright colours and I

82

don't see why I should have to be unsuitably dressed just because I'm hard up.'

'So what it boils down to is that everyone else has got to make sacrifices, but not you?'

Christine started to cry again. 'What a beastly thing to say, Martha! I don't know how you can be so mean, knowing how wretched I am. And you're a fine one to talk! I wouldn't be half so badly off, if it wasn't for all that money you're getting from Derek and I bet he wouldn't have given it to you, if he'd known you'd turn so nasty.'

Martha was so stunned by these accusations that it took her some time to formulate a reply. Finally, she said, 'I'm not absolutely sure that I follow you, Christine. It's true that Derek very kindly promised to make me an allowance and I was very grateful, but I haven't had a penny of it yet and, quite honestly, I didn't expect to now.'

'There you go again! What a horrid thing to say! As though I'd try to cheat you out of it! Anyway, I couldn't, could I?'

'I see no reason why not.'

'You mean he didn't tell you? Charles was certain he had. You honestly don't know?'

'Know what?'

'That Derek made a new will when he was in London. He's left you fifty thousand pounds.'

WEDNESDAY, 15th AUGUST

The Jury returned an Open Verdict, largely as a result of one surprising piece of evidence, which conflicted with straightforward Death by Misadventure.

This had nothing to do with the disconnected telephone, which was touched on and then, to Billy's relief, dismissed with practically no comment. It was rather that, contrary to the understanding of everyone except the police, the staircase had not collapsed under Derek Marsh's tremendous weight. The three top steps had been sawn through and removed, leaving a gaping hole of about four square feet. There was absolutely no way of accounting for this and no one who would admit responsibility.

Cafferty, when called upon by the Coroner to offer an explanation, was at his blandest, stating that the deed must have been done between Friday evening and the time of the accident, for, as God was his witness, he had checked every mortal thing, as indeed he always did, before his men packed it in for the weekend and he was ready to swear on his oath that there had been nothing wrong with the staircase then. Looking exaggeratedly wide-eyed and innocent, he ventured to suggest that, since the house was open to every prowler with sufficient strength to pull aside a plastic sheet, this was doubtless the devilish work of some outsider who, thinking to help himself to a bit of free firewood, had been disturbed in the act and made off.

He ran into difficulties at this point because the Coroner

84

wanted to know why, if this was the case, a saw had been left in full view of any passer-by with enough curiosity to glance through a front window. After the self-righteousness which had gone before, Cafferty was obviously reluctant to admit that it was due to sheer carelessness and, rather late in the day, had managed to dredge up the information that none of the men had claimed this particular saw as his property.

'And the odd thing is,' Billy recalled later, 'that, for the first time in the proceedings, I was inclined to believe him. You can always tell when Cafferty's lying, but, being such a stranger to the truth, he is apt to express it rather clumsily.'

'Tubby was quite pleased with the verdict, I have to tell you,' said Avril, who was a JP and well in with the police.

'Well, I'm afraid I'm not,' Martha admitted, 'although it could have been worse, I suppose. Curiously enough, it was the sawing part which convinced me that it must have been an accident and I can't understand why it bothered the jury so much.'

'Can't you? Then I'll explain. It planted the seed of an idea that it might have been done purposely to bring about someone's death.'

'I can see that, of course, and it's the whole point. I confess I've been worried because it did seem to me that things were looking bad for Tim. That threesome of theirs was just the kind of set-up which would prejudice country people against him and, since he was the last person to have seen Derek alive, I shouldn't have been all that surprised if they'd brought in a verdict of murder and named him. But, of course, they couldn't swallow the idea, any more than I can, of two men walking into an empty house together, whereupon one of them brandishes a saw and starts hacking away at the staircase. After which, the second man obligingly stands in position to be pushed through the gap. It's too ludicrous for even our local dimwits to credit.'

'What if the sawing part had been done in advance, though?' Avril suggested. 'That would have simplified things considerably.'

'It can't have been much in advance, otherwise surely there would have been a grave risk of the wrong person getting killed?'

'And perhaps the wrong person did get killed? Have you thought of that?'

'Oh no, really,' Billy protested. 'Why do you both have to make everything so complicated? Why not just accept the obvious?'

'If we knew what that was.'

'That one of the carpenters, knowing the staircase was scheduled for demolition, thought he'd make a start on it and Cafferty either doesn't know which one it was, or is covering up for him.'

'My dear boy, I don't call that obvious, in the least. It leaves far too many loose ends. There's not only the mystery of the telephone now, there's also one extra saw to be accounted for.'

'Yes, but if anyone had really used it to commit a murder, would he then be so careless as to leave it lying around?'

'Why not? Much simpler than lugging it away and finding another hiding place. In fact, I don't call it careless at all, I think it was rather clever. Most people would assume, probably now do assume, in view of the tangle Cafferty made of explaining it, that it belonged to one of his men. Though I doubt if Tubby does.'

'Speaking of that,' Martha interrupted, 'how do you

favour the idea that the real reason for Cafferty becoming confused at that point was not the one Billy gave us, but because he had done the deed himself?'

'Well, that's a novel idea! What do you say, Billy? Does he make a practice of murdering the clients?'

'No, no, Avril, I wasn't suggesting he was a murderer and I wasn't thinking of Derek, as it happens. It goes back to what we were saying about the wrong person having fallen. You see, Cafferty couldn't have known about the meeting which had been arranged at the Farm on Sunday morning. It was a last-minute appointment, fixed up on Saturday between you and Derek. Isn't that so, Billy?'

'Quite correct. Cafferty didn't know about it, and so what?'

'It just occurred to me that he might have believed the most likely person to have been prowling around during the weekend was Dolly.'

This theory, evidently put forward in all seriousness, quite stunned her audience and even Avril was rendered speechless, although naturally the first to recover.

'Well, that takes the bun, Martha! Can you be right, I wonder? We all suspected there was something fishy about Dolly's accident and I should never be surprised if Cafferty knew more about it than he let on. Yes, that may well be the answer.'

'Oh, what nonsense are you two women hatching now? He may be a crook, in his own small way, but he's not a murdering lunatic and I assure you it wouldn't have needed a solid bulk like Derek for that fall to be fatal. Twelve feet, head first, on to a stone floor, may I remind you? A frail old lady would have had even less chance of survival. No, I simply won't have it. Besides,' he went on, opening his eyes briefly, 'there's something you've both forgotten. So far as Cafferty knew, Dolly was incarcerated in hospital, with no possibility of getting out. She was the last person he would have expected to be snooping around Bookers during the weekend.'

'Although, as I've told you, I have a nasty feeling that's exactly what she was doing,' Martha said thoughtfully. 'Still, you're right, Billy. Cafferty couldn't possibly have foreseen such a thing. I'm sorry if I maligned him, it's just that it would be so nice if we could somehow convince ourselves that Derek's death had been simply an unlucky accident.'

'In any case, I think we'll wait a bit before we pass your theory on to Tubby,' Avril said. 'It wouldn't really suit us if he were to arrest Cafferty before the house is finished, would it, Billy?'

'Given the evidence, so far, I shouldn't think that's very likely, would you?'

'No, but now he's got the green light, nothing's going to stop him plugging away until he's arrested somebody, so it's important to keep him on the right lines, in my opinion.'

' 'Specially as I now have to be counted among the suspects,' Martha reminded her.

< 2 >

Four miles away, Christine Marsh had just entered the bar of the Beresford Court Hotel, where Tim Whitfield was already drinking with another man at one of the tables. She had removed her black straw hat, but still wore the black and white silk dress, which was part of the new consignment from London, and delivered in the nick of time for the inquest.

The man Tim was talking to had also been at the inquest,

but standing at the back of the courtroom, and she had not been aware of him. All the same, at first sight, his presence induced a distinctly disagreeable shock. Walking into a room and finding two men waiting for her was so much the pattern of her life that, in a dreamlike way, it semed that the thread had never been broken. The added fact that on this occasion one was Tim and the other a stout and broad-shouldered man added an element of nightmare to the situation. For one devastating moment she really believed he was Derek.

The moment passed because when he stood up to greet her she saw that, as well as being a good four inches shorter than Derek, his features were neater and chubbier too, and that he had round blue eyes and a small scrubbing-brush moustache. Where one had been elephantine, the other was a teddy bear.

'Hallo, Chris! Let me introduce Mr Wiseman . . . Mrs Marsh . . . who's been kind enough to keep me company. I was telling him about the house and your idea of dividing it into two. He's lived in these parts for years and can put us on to some really go-ahead estate agents, if we need advice on how to go about it.'

'Oh yes, how interesting!' Christine answered coolly, making a great business of smoothing out her gloves and laying them beside her on the banquette. 'It's a glorious part of the world, isn't it, Mr Wiseman? Only just over an hour's drive from town and yet so completely unspoilt.'

She was not best pleased by this development, being far from certain that she wished her idea of dividing the house to be taken up with quite such alacrity, and furthermore she rather deplored Tim's habit of getting into conversation with anyone who so much as wished him good evening. It had not mattered in Africa, where Europeans fell into a few easily recognisable categories, but these things were not so well ordered in the UK. She could not quite trust him, or herself either, to distinguish accurately between the travelling salesman and the Chairman of the Board.

However, despite the 'Mr', this one had all the hall-marks of a retired colonel, or someone of that type, so he was probably all right, and this impression soon received comforting support from the demeanour of the waiter who hurried over to take their order. Far from the stony stare which Tim's finger-clicking performance usually drew from him, he arrived at the double and did everything except actually prostrate himself when Mr Wiseman said Yes, thank you kindly, he would have another whisky; with water and no ice, if you please.

'Yes,' he said again, turning back to Christine, 'I agree with you there. Can't beat it. But then I'm a Sussex man, myself, so I suppose you could say I was prejudiced.'

'And have you lived here all your life?'

'Off and on, you know. I spent a few years overseas during the war and I had a spell in India in my young days. Never got to Africa, I'm sorry to say, unless you count going ashore at Cape Town for twenty-four hours. I gather that was your home until recently? Must have been a splendid life out there.'

'Used to be,' Tim said. 'Things have gone a bit downhill recently.'

'Oh, really? Sorry to hear that. In what way?'

'Just a general falling off of standards, so to speak. The old African peasant is still a good chap, loyal as they come, but they've got some pretty funny blokes in the top jobs.'

'Is that so?' Mr Wiseman asked, looking saddened by this news. 'Well, that's progress, so they tell me.'

'If you can call it progress,' Christine remarked with a toss of the head. 'Personally, I don't. They'll be back where

90

they started in one generation, in my opinion. Apart from the railways and refrigerators, there'll be nothing to show that we were ever there.'

'Bad as that, is it? No wonder you decided to cut loose and get out. Don't blame you, really.'

It was the first time since her arrival in the UK that Christine had encountered such a sympathetic audience. In her experience, most people got a glazed look in their eyes as soon as Africa was mentioned and their one desire seemed to be to dash on to another subject with all possible speed. Mr Wiseman was different. He was evidently a man of the world, who had led an interesting and adventurous life of his own and was therefore eager to hear about the interesting and adventurous lives of others.

'That was partly why we decided to leave,' she told him gravely. 'We'd have stuck it out, if we could, you know, mainly for the sake of the people who worked on our estate. They were utterly dependent on us, in every way; and their families too. Unfortunately, that caused resentment among certain people who wanted all the power for themselves and they had rather unpleasant ways of venting their feelings.'

'Good God! You don't mean . . . actual violence?'

"Fraid so, old man,' Tim said, enjoying himself quite as much as Christine. 'Not so bad for us chaps, of course, but one didn't awfully care for the thought of the little woman being in danger.'

'I should think not, indeed! And things had really got to that pitch, had they?'

'They really had. I can take a certain amount of risk in my stride,' Christine told him, with a plucky little smile, 'but when it comes to sleeping with a gun under your pillow every night, I can't say I awfully enjoy it.'

'You amaze me! To think of one's own kith and kin

having to endure such a state of affairs! It just shows how ignorant one is about what goes on outside one's own backyard! But you managed to escape any . . . er . . . actual unpleasantness, I hope?'

'Oh yes, we were pretty lucky, on the whole,' Tim said, and then, as Christine also started to speak, glanced at her quickly with an expression which might have signified a warning of some kind. Mr Wiseman, who was looking down into his glass, as though vaguely disappointed to find it empty, did not appear to notice this.

'Forgive me,' he said, looking up again. 'Mustn't speak out of turn. Probably rather a painful subject. I can quite understand. I remember once when I was in Pindi. We were living under canvas at the time. Friend of mine got stabbed while he was asleep in his tent. Fearful shock, it was. I don't think I shall ever get it out of my mind. But it was a long time before I could bring myself to talk about it.'

'How perfectly ghastly! Did they catch the man who did it?'

'Oh yes, in the end, after he'd done a bit more damage. He'd gone berserk, of course. Didn't make things any easier for the rest of us, though.'

'No, I'm sure it didn't,' Christine said, leaning forward and speaking with great intensity, 'and I can well understand your feelings because something of the same kind happened to us. One of our own servants was involved, a man we thought we could trust implicitly; but he'd got into the hands of a witch doctor, who'd filled him up with all that mumbo jumbo they go in for.'

'Wicked, isn't it? Mean to tell me this fellow of yours killed someone too?'

'No, but it was a near thing. It was my husband he tried to attack, as it happened. Luckily, he . . .'

'Hallo, hallo, hallo,' Tim broke in, raising his right arm. 'What's this I see? Empty glasses all round? Can't have that, can we?'

'No, no, my dear fellow, this is my round, I absolutely insist. Now, what are you both having? Same again?'

'No more for me, thank you,' Christine said primly. 'It's been a difficult day and I think it's time for dinner and an early night.'

'Sure? How about you, sir?'

'No, I think Chris is right. Thanks all the same.'

'Too bad. Still, I ought to be toddling too, I suppose. And perhaps you'll let me return your hospitality some other time. Will you be staying here long?'

'Oh yes, indefinitely; well, that is, until the house is ready,' Christine said, holding out her hand. 'We'll look forward to meeting you again.'

'Me too. Often drop in around this time. So I'll say au revoir. It's been a pleasure talking to you.'

'Au revoir,' Christine said graciously, then muttered, as Mr Wiseman walked away, 'Why did you kick me like that?'

Tim looked at her unhappily. 'Sorry, old girl, I just thought . . . well . . . you were running on a bit, you know.'

'What if I was? We've nothing to hide, have we?'

'No, of course not; but, I mean to say, we don't know the first thing about him, do we?'

'We know he's an intelligent, agreeable person, and a gentleman, which is more than you can say for most people you meet in this country now.'

'Well, yes, I expect you're right. He seemed a harmless enough old buffer, as you say.'

There was an interval while he tried once more to attract the waiter's attention; but his heart was not in it and he soon returned to his empty glass, tilting it back and forth, as he said, 'Rawalpindi is not in India, is it? I always thought it was in Pakistan.'

'So it is.'

'He said he'd been in India and yet he was talking about Pindi.'

Christine gave a little trill of laughter. 'Really, Tim, fancy worrying about that! Of course, Rawalpindi is in Pakistan now, but Mr Wiseman was talking about something which took place when he was a young man. It was long before Partition, I dare say. In the days of the good old Raj, no doubt.'

'Oh yes, what a clot! Sorry, Chris!'

So delighted was she by this display of superior knowledge that she temporarily forgot her sorrows and directed a radiant smile at the waiter, spreading her hands in a gesture of mock despair; and he, who had been studiously ignoring them for five minutes, capitulated at once and hurried over to take their order. When he returned with the tray of fresh drinks, she leant towards him, still smiling, though in a more subdued and suffering way and said, 'The gentleman who was with us just now, I imagine he's a well known character around here?'

'Yes, Madam, extremely well known.'

'I thought so. And my guess is that he's a retired Army man. Am I right?'

'Could have been, once upon a time, I dare say, but there's nothing retired about him now.'

'Oh?'

'Chief Superintendent is what he is now. Detective Chief Superintendent Wiseman. Old Tubby, they call him behind his back.'

THURSDAY, 16th AUGUST

'I've brought you a bottle of wine, Martha. Hope it's not too dry for you?'

'How very kind of you, Tubby! No, indeed it's not. Dry sherry is the only kind I like. Also it won't be such a temptation for Dolly. She prefers the syrupy kind. I hope you can stay and drink some of it?'

'Might as well. Must be getting on for midday. Here, let me open it for you.'

'So you've got Dolly back with you, have you?' he asked, when she returned with two sherry glasses.

'Not yet, but she's coming this afternoon. I'm to fetch her at three. It was going to be rather a problem, with Adrian here as well, but luckily Billy Jones has very kindly offered to put him up for a week or two. He seems to think it will be less trouble for him than having Miranda on her own and tidying up after him all the time. Otherwise, I don't quite see how I could have managed, with Dolly in the state she is.'

'Still on the sick list, is she?'

'Well no, I wouldn't quite put it like that,' Martha replied in her most worried voice. 'Her arm is still in plaster, of course, so she can't dress herself or anything, which won't make life any easier, but in a general way her health is better than it was before the accident. It's done her good, being in hospital, and they've given her some therapy treatment which has worked wonders. I've never seen her so calm and sensible as she was a few days ago.'

'Was?'

'Well, that was before she heard about her son-in-law's death, you see; before any of us heard. It was on Sunday morning, as a matter of fact, when I called in. Christine had already been to see her and she was so bright and cheerful, but in a rational way, if you know what I mean?'

'So her daughter had been, had she? There are rumours that she's not always over-conscientious about visiting her.'

'They're true, I'm afraid. Of course, she's had a lot to cope with, over the house and everything, even before Derek's accident, but sometimes she did rather neglect poor old Dolly. That was why I tried to look in at least once a day. Of course, if I'd been certain Christine would be able to manage it on Sunday, I needn't have bothered. It wasn't terribly convenient, with Adrian's lunch to cook and so on. She told me she'd try and fit in a visit to the hospital, but unfortunately one can't always depend on her.'

'But at least the two of you didn't overlap, I take it?'

'No, she was ahead of me, as it happens. I met Matron in the hall and she told me Christine had just left and that she'd spoken to her about sending Dolly home, now that there'd been such a steady improvement, and I must confess that when I saw her I had to agree. But it was a very different story when I was there yesterday.'

'You mean she's taking it hard about her son-in-law's death?'

'My dear Tubby, you've no conception! We're right back where we started. Worse, if anything. I can't understand it either. I mean, naturally, she's grieved for Christine's sake, but I can't see why that should be enough to send

96

her so completely off the rails. She only met Derek about twice in her life.'

'Well, she was never very strong in the head, was she? It doesn't take much to rock that boat. Can I give you a drop more sherry?'

'Oh, my dear Tubby, I am so sorry! Please do help yourself. And me too, just a very little. It's so delicious, but I mustn't have too much, it always makes me so garrulous.'

'Nothing wrong with that. I suppose the sad fact is,' he went on, having poured a full glass for each of them, 'that this so-called cure didn't get to the heart of the matter. Just the result of a change of scene and being a bit of a heroine and so on. Wouldn't have lasted, even if things had gone normally, I dare say.'

'Yes, I agree, in a way, but on the other hand it's such a complete reversal. Just now she's more childish and irrational than I've ever known her. And there's usually some very transparent reason for these bad turns.'

'But you said yourself that Marsh's death had hit her pretty hard. What better reason do you need?'

'Oh, I don't know, Tubby, but, to be honest with you, other people's troubles don't usually impinge very much. It's more often when she's done something naughty or foolish herself and is suffering either from guilty conscience or fear of being found out.'

'Like carving up a staircase? Oh, come on now, Martha! That's going a bit far! The old girl's a sight too tottery for games like that, isn't she?'

'Tubby, how dare you? I may be in my cups, but I know perfectly well that I never so much as hinted at such a thing.'

'No, no, of course you didn't, but I'm not so blind that I can't see you've got something on your mind and, whether you realise it or not, you're implying that you fear there may be some connection between Dolly's current state of mind and what happened to Derek Marsh. If so, you can take heart, because I think I may be able to talk you out of it.'

'I'm sure I hope so, Tubby. You see, it's not that I believe for one moment that she's really malicious, or would wish to cause serious harm to anyone. It's just that she does get these extraordinary fixations. For instance, she's always maintained that the foreman at the building site was directly responsible for her accident and I can't quite rid myself of the notion that she might have tried to pay him out, if you see what I mean?'

'Yes, I do see what you mean. So that he would tumble downstairs and bump his head? But I said I could ease your mind and I can. Whether the staircase was damaged with malice aforethought or not, it can only have been done on Saturday, or very early on Sunday morning.'

'Ah!'

'So, you see, Dolly can have had no hand in it.'

'No.'

'Is that the best you can do? You don't sound very cheerful.'

'I'm not.'

'So what's the trouble now? This is purely unofficial, I should remind you.'

'I know that, but the verdict was such an unsatisfactory one, in my opinion. It does nothing to stop the gossip and rumour.'

'And, despite what I've told you, you still believe your aunt may have had something to do with it?'

'The trouble is, you see, Tubby,' Martha said unhappily, 'I have reason to believe she may have been at Bookers

Farm on Saturday afternoon,' and she proceeded to tell him about the car she had seen driving away.

'What worries me most,' she concluded, 'is that, if she was there and saw someone, or anything at all suspicious, there'll be no holding her. Once she gets over her fright, it will be all round the neighbourhood. And that's not going to make it very pleasant for the rest of us.'

'How can you tell it was one of Lubbock's cars you saw?'

'I recognised it. We sometimes have to hire one from him when mine is out of action. Besides, I saw the driver clearly. He was wearing one of those shiny, peaked caps.'

'I see. Well, we can soon find out if you're right.'

'How? I hope you're not suggesting that I should come straight out with it and ask her? You don't know much about Dolly, if you believe that would provide any solution.'

'No, but there's nothing to stop us having a quiet word with Lubbock, is there? Or, if you feel it would be undignified to appear to be spying on her, why not begin by asking Mrs Marsh? If she's been more attentive lately, she may be able to throw some light on what her mother was up to on Saturday.'

'No, she won't. Christine was in London all that day, and Tim too. They didn't get back until dinner time. I think they went to a theatre and Christine had to see about her new clothes.'

'Oh, yes? I thought she looked very well turned out at the inquest. Not quite the class of our local dress shops.'

'No, she goes to some place in Knightsbridge, near the hotel where they all stayed. Do you really think I should be wise to ask Lubbock, Tubby? I shall feel worse than ever if I'm proved right.'

'Well, that's a risk you'll have to take, Martha, but I

should say it was worth taking because, personally, I'm firmly of the opinion that you're letting your imagination run riot. I should think your real problem is how you're going to cope with Dolly when you've got her back. Whatever the cause of it, if she goes on being so excitable and upset, you're going to have a hard job with her, aren't you?'

'It won't be easy,' Martha agreed, 'and I confess that I rather dread facing all that turmoil again, but it won't be quite such a problem in future. Clever Dr Mead has very kindly roped in a woman to help. She's married, with grown-up children, but she trained as a nurse and she'll be able to come in for an hour or so most days. You see, I can afford it now.'

'Well, that's good news indeed!'

'Derek left me fifty thousand pounds. Didn't you know? I thought the news would be all round the place by now.'

'Oh, I heard something about it. Didn't realise it was so much, though. Congratulations, Martha! No more than you deserve, of course, after what you've put up with for all these years.'

'Won't you have another drink to celebrate?'

'No, thanks. I've got half a bottle of Moselle waiting for me with my lunch.'

'I expect it will be months and months before the estate is settled,' she explained, as they walked out to his car, 'but the bank is perfectly willing to advance me whatever I need. Isn't it incredible? I simply can't get used to the idea of affluence. I keep expecting someone to tell me that it was all a joke.'

'How was the rest of the money left, do you know?'

'Oh, I think Christine gets the income for her lifetime and a fairly hefty lump sum as well. She pretends not to know how much, but enough to pay for the house, I gather. The rest is left in trust for Adrian, on her death.'

'Is that so?'

'Yes, and she's complaining about that, too. I must say, it was rather an odd thing to have done, but of course he had no children of his own and he was an unusual man, in some ways.'

'So it seems. I dare say he had his reasons.'

'Which reminds me, Tubby. Aren't you going to tell me what you really came for?' she asked, as he unlocked the car door. 'I'm sure it wasn't just to bring me that nice present.'

'Oh, I like giving good wine to people who appreciate it; and I always enjoy a chat with you, Martha.'

'Rather too chatty this time, I'm afraid. I shall probably be regretting it by this evening.'

He looked a little like Winnie the Pooh, as he heaved and squeezed his portly person in behind the steering wheel, and the resemblance was heightened when, having sat perfectly still for a minute, to regain his breath, he began to sing a little song, as he watched Martha walk back to the cottage. It was a cheerful enough tune, but the words were not particularly inspired.

'I wonder? I wonder? I WONDER?' he warbled all the way home to his half-bottle of Moselle.

< 2 >

No merry songs came bubbling up from Adrian, for he had troubles by the score. In addition to the haunting, ever-present guilt over his unfaithfulness to Diana, he was distinctly worried by the fact that the police had been trampling all over Bookers Farm and, no doubt, turning

101

the place upside down. Reason told him that his secret must still be safe, since otherwise he would surely have heard about it, but he was growing increasingly obsessed by the need to make quite certain of this and, like a true criminal, to revisit the scene of his crime.

He had actually made one half-hearted attempt to do so, on the day after the inquest, but Cafferty had not been cooperative. In fact, he had been in a foul temper and, short of commanding Adrian to get lost, had done everything in his power to foil him. Furthermore, it had turned out that there was a man working on the very spot which he most needed to investigate, so he could have saved himself the bother of coming at all, as well as the ticking off from Cafferty.

The only way round the problem, and it should have presented itself as a simple one, was to pay another visit to the Farm after dusk, when the builders had packed up and gone, but he was forced to invent all sorts of reasons why it would be impractical to do this, because he did not care to acknowledge that he was scared of being there, on his own, in the twilight.

As though these fears and uncertainties were not racking enough, he was also gravely worried about his new stereo record-player and tape-recorder. He had boasted quite a lot about these to Miranda during the evening they had spent together on the night of Avril's dinner party, and since then she had asked him once or twice, in an unpleasantly patronising way, when he was going to give her a demonstration. Failure to comply had unfortunately withered her interest instead of stimulating it, and now, when he mentioned the subject, she only laughed and looked at him with a pitying expression.

This was almost unendurable because, although he very rarely received expensive presents and had been known to compensate for this by bragging about possessions which, in fact, had only been vaguely promised for some indefinite time in the future, on this occasion he had been speaking the unvarnished truth. His mother really had bought him the most super record-player and tape-machine, with every imaginable attachment the heart could wish for.

The big snag was that she had now become suspiciously evasive about it. He had consented to leave it behind at the hotel when he moved in with Aunt Martha, because even he was forced to recognise that there wasn't room for it at the cottage, but, on learning of his impending transfer to the Jones's house, where space abounded, his very first request had been for his beloved toy to be restored to him.

It was then that his mother had started making excuses for not handing it over and bewilderment had gradually given way to gnawing anxiety, as it was borne in on him that she had other plans for its disposal and no one knew better than he did what they were most likely to be. Since, from within the first hour of learning of his stepfather's death, she had rarely ceased to moan about her financial ruin and to threaten him with imminent starvation, not to mention forced labour as an errand boy (although he was not quite sure what these were, or whether they existed outside her imagination), any fool could guess that what she really had in mind for the beloved toy was to flog it.

Fortunately, the situation was not yet desperate, for he was already at work on a plan to outwit her. The success of it hinged on various premises being correct and he was rather proud at having arrived at these by a psychological process. In the first place, he was fairly certain that she would not try to sell it locally, for she would not wish the neighbourhood shopkeepers to know about her dire financial straits, however relentlessly she might impress them on her own family. Secondly, it would also be out of character for her to tout it round the London shops in person, and it was equally improbable that she knew of anyone to whom to apply for advice.

Putting all these factors together, he had reached the conclusion that her most likely move would be to make enquiries at the store where they had bought the thing in the first place and to consult them about her chances in the second-hand market. In order to plug up this hole in advance, he had already written to the shop to ask for information about second-hand machines of this make, enclosing a stamped, addressed envelope. The original transaction had been made in Christine's name and, not for the first time in his life, he was thankful that his was Whitfield and not Marsh.

Having completed these preliminaries, he concentrated on the main operation, waiting only for his mother to announce that his father would be driving her to London on the following Monday for what she described as 'a working lunch' with Charles Lawson, to put the finishing touches to it.

This required a little help from Miranda and she was not immediately disposed to cooperate.

'Why all the subterfuge?' she asked. 'Why not just say you want it right away?'

This was not the way things got done, in Adrian's experience, and he said, as though explaining to a child, 'Because it wouldn't work. She doesn't want me to have it and she'd only invent some excuse, like it would be a nuisance for your father, or something.'

'And he could say it wouldn't be a nuisance. I'll tell him to, if you like.'

'Oh, can't you understand, Miranda? It wouldn't do any good. She'd only dream up some other excuse. Listen, all I want from you is the getaway car. You don't have to come inside with me. Just turn the car round while I'm casing the joint, and don't forget to keep the engine running. It could be quite exciting, actually.'

'It doesn't excite me. I find it thoroughly childish and, what's more, I don't think you'd get away with it.'

'Why not? It'll be dead simple.'

'That's what you say!'

'I've done much riskier things than this, if you want to know.'

'I don't want to know. For a start, I think you make most of it up.'

'All right, listen to this, then. Once, when she was going out to dinner, she took her jewellery out of the safe and forgot to lock it up again, and when she'd gone I took twenty pounds out of the envelope where they kept their cash.'

'What on earth for?'

'Well, you know, for fun, really.'

'Were you caught?'

'No, she always thought one of the house-boys must have pinched it. Luckily for me, one of them sloped off back to his village soon afterwards and the police said it must have been him who took the money. It all worked out fantastically well.'

'Well, I think you must be out of your mind, but I suppose I'll tag along, if it means so much to you. Only don't get any ideas about a Bonnie and Clyde act with me, because it's not on. I happen to be fairly law abiding.'

'Oh, there's nothing illegal about it this time,' he said hastily. 'I just told you that as an example. All I'm doing now is collecting something which belongs to me and they all know me at the hotel, so they won't raise an eyebrow. That bit about the getaway car was only a joke. I thought you knew that. It weighs a ton, though, so we'll need your car to get it away in.'

'And what happens when your mother comes back and finds it gone?'

'Nothing.'

'Is that so? From what I've heard, I'd rather expect her to have forty-nine hysterical fits.'

'So she will, in private, but she can't very well get me put in prison for stealing, can she? And she'd look pretty silly if she made a scene about the receptionist handing over her key. After all, I am her son and I only came to fetch something which they knew was mine.'

Miranda, who only had the haziest recollection of her own mother and, as a breed, was inclined to regard them as largely superfluous, had nevertheless imagined boys to hold a softer attitude and was rather intrigued by Adrian's ruthless detachment.

'Don't you like her at all?' she asked.

'Oh sure, she's okay,' he muttered, turning his head away as he felt the tears stinging his eyes. 'At least, she used to be when I was small. But she sent me away to a boarding school when I was six and after that it was all different. She said it was because the climate where we lived wasn't suitable for European children, but it wasn't that at all. My stepfather made her do it. He always hated my guts and he couldn't wait to get me out of the way. And he changed my mother completely.'

'Well, now he's dead, perhaps she'll change back again?'

'Hope so, but it won't happen in time to give me back what belongs to me. Listen, are you on, or not?'

'Like I said. If it means so much to you.'

'Oh, whacko, Miranda, that's great! And we'll set it up in your old nursery. I can't wait for you to see it!'

106

FRIDAY, 17th AUGUST

About twenty-four hours after Adrian and Miranda had completed their plans for the grand snatch, a personable young man in a brown suit walked into a Knightsbridge boutique and asked if he might have a word with the Manageress. He had a friendly, well-scrubbed look about him and hair that was neither conspicuously long, nor conspicuously short. He might have been an accountant, or an Assistant Bank Manager; in fact, he was making enquiries about a stolen credit card.

It was just after two o'clock and he was told that Mrs Grayson was still out to lunch, which, from his point of view, was entirely satisfactory. Manageresses, he had reason to believe, were liable to be tougher propositions than those junior members of the staff who were expected to eat their lunch between twelve and one, and he earnestly hoped to conclude his business before Mrs Grayson returned.

'Then I wonder if you could help me, by any chance?' he asked in his modest, engaging way, which was not wholly assumed for the occasion, for the girl he was addressing was exactly his cup of tea. Besides being pretty enough to eat, she looked sufficiently bright to answer his questions intelligently, while sufficiently inexperienced not to delve too deeply into his qualifications for asking them.

'I will, if I can,' she replied, smiling back and delighting him still further. 'A credit card, you say?'

'Like this,' he said, opening his wallet and bringing out one of the international variety. 'It appears to have been stolen several days ago from a Mrs Marsh, who was staying at the hotel across the road, and we are trying to get a description of the thief, who is a woman, obviously. I was wondering if, by any chance, you had recently had a customer of that name, or rather, pretending to be of that name. You see, these people normally operate in the immediate area, that is to say, make several quick purchases and then discard — Oh, Lord! What a ghastly pun! — throw away the card, very often before its absence has been discovered. I've been tramping up and down, trying all the likely shops, but so far no luck. This is about my last shot.'

Even before he made his little joke he had seen from her expression that he was on the right track, but he carried on to the end because he wanted her to feel sorry for him, as well as interested in his problem.

'Did you say Marsh?' she asked. 'Well, strange as it may seem, I do believe I can help you. She wasn't my client, but I remember her well because she created quite a sensation.'

'Oh dear,' the young man said. 'That doesn't sound much like it, I'm afraid. The usual pattern is to be as unobtrusive as possible. It's not part of their game to draw attention to themselves. What kind of sensation?'

'She was, oh, you know, the fussy type. One of those who tried on practically everything in the shop and complained about the lot. That sort very often walks out without buying a single thing and you spend half an hour putting it all back on the rails again, but this Mrs Marsh wasn't one of those. In fact, it was quite a big order.'

'Well, that sounds a bit more hopeful.'

'Would you like me to look up the details? As I told you, she wasn't my client, but I expect I can find them, if you'll hang on for a minute.'

'There's something else I'd rather ask you first, since you've been so awfully kind and helpful. You are certain this woman called herself Mrs Marsh?'

'Oh, definitely. There was quite a lot of talk about her in the shop when she'd gone and I remembered the name because it seemed to suit her so well. She had that sort of bronze colouring, which reminded me of marsh marigolds, and it kind of stuck. I often do that, actually. You know, associate names with colours and things, to help me remember them.'

'So do I. It's called mnemonics, I believe.'

'Gosh, is it really? I must remember that. The thing is, how am I going to find a mnemonics for mnemonics?'

'That's a problem, isn't it? Anyway, I'm willing to bet that was the last you saw of the so-called Mrs Marsh.'

'Well, no,' she said doubtfully, evidently wavering between the truth and her desire not to disappoint him. 'Far from it, I'm afraid. You see, nearly everything she bought had to be altered. I told you she was fussy beyond belief and when the things were ready she wouldn't have them posted, she insisted on coming in to fit them all first.'

'Oh, no!' he said, looking very crestfallen. 'Are you sure you're not mixing her up with someone else?'

'Absolutely positive. I'm most awfully sorry, but the fact is that I have a very good reason for remembering that occasion too.'

'What, more mnemonics?'

'No, it's engraved on my heart, but for a different reason. It was Saturday morning, you see. We're often frantically busy then, but this was a specially quiet one. Well, you know, August and the sale's over and everything. It's a frightful drag, standing around with nothing to do. You get so that you could rush into the street and pull the customers in by brute force; but at least that day we thought we'd close on time for once and get away at a civilised hour. And then, twenty minutes to one and what do you know? In waltzes Mrs Marsh, fresh as a daisy and wanting to try on every last garment before she pays her bill. Her husband, if that's who he was, got quite embarrassed about it.'

'Could you describe him, by the way? Every little helps in a case like this and it might give us a pointer.'

'Well, he was quite a bit older than her, I'd say. Going grey . . . not much to look at, but quite a pleasant sort of face.'

'Tall? Short?'

'On the short side, and he had this short, crinkly hair. He smiled a lot, I remember, but I think it was embarrassment, really. And why not? It was well past one when they left.'

'By which time you were all so fed up that the saleswoman who served her wasn't too particular about checking her identity and so on? Right?'

'Well, no,' the girl said, looking dismayed again at having to let him down. 'It wasn't a bit like that. It was Mrs Grayson herself, you see, and she's a demon for that kind of thing. She wouldn't have let anything past her, if it had meant keeping us all here till midnight.'

'Yes, I see. And did the customer then take everything away with her?'

'Not everything, no. One or two of them still didn't come up to scratch. But she went out wearing one of the dresses and jacket because she said she was going to the theatre and it would be just right for that. I think she took about half the other things with her, including a hat, which she said might get crushed in the post, and we sent the rest to an address in the country. The reason why I know that is because getting off the parcels is one of my jobs. I'm not being much help to you, am I?'

'On the contrary, Miss . . . ?'

'Susan's my name.'

'And I'm Frank. I hope you don't need a mnemonic for that. I was going to say: on the contrary, you've been a tremendous help and I couldn't be more grateful, but you know what?'

'No.'

'I have an awful feeling that your Mrs Marsh isn't the one we're after at all. She sounds like the genuine article, from your description. Pity she forgot to tell us she made all these purchases before the card was stolen, but there you are! All in the day's work. All the same, I'm the one who should be apologising, for taking up so much of your time. And all for nothing, as it turns out.'

'That's all right. No bother at all.'

'Well, thanks very much,' he said, picking up his hat and then pausing to stare at it as intently as though it held the key to the mysteries of the universe. 'I suppose you wouldn't . . . No, of course not.'

'What?'

Her tone was still friendly, but she had assumed the wary expression of one whose encounters with strange men invariably concluded with an enquiry as to whether she was doing anything special that evening.

'Wouldn't what?'

'Well, you've been so helpful and you're obviously madly observant. This is probably a stupid question, but I just wondered whether, by any chance, you'd picked up any idea about which theatre your Mrs Marsh was going to that afternoon. She didn't happen to mention anything about it, I suppose?'

'Oh! Oh, I see. No, I don't think she did.'

'No, silly question, really. It's just that I have to, you know, bash out some kind of report to my boss and it struck me that, well, you know, if she had happened to mention which theatre it was, I could go along there and do a bit more checking up. It would sort of round the thing off, if you see what I mean? Never mind, it can't be helped. And thanks again, I'm more than grateful.'

'Hang on!' Susan said. 'I don't know what your secret is, but you're fantastic at bringing out the total recall. It could just possibly have been either the Criterion or the Savoy. Several others, as well, I dare say, but I'd certainly put those two on your list.'

'You really do have the most amazing brain,' he said, absent-mindedly dropping his hat back on the table. 'It's simply fascinating the way it works. Do tell me why you think it might have been one of those two? They don't even sound alike, or begin with the same letter.'

'Oh no, it's nothing like that, but, you see, clothes are my trade and I remember that she wore the yellow and green sleeveless silk dress with matching jacket when she went out. It made her look even more marigoldy, actually, but she chose it because it was the coolest and you know why that was?'

'No, but I can't wait to hear.'

'Because the theatre they were going to was underground. "In the bowels of the earth" was how she described it and so it was bound to be stiflingly hot. I don't know how many theatres there are like that in London, but I do know that the Savoy and Criterion are two of them.'

'Well, it's worth a try and you're a genius. I can't thank you enough.'

'Oh, that's all right, it's been fun. Amazing what you can dredge up, once you get started. Think I'll make a good witness, if I ever have to appear at the Old Bailey?'

'Yes,' he agreed, smiling at her with deep amusement, 'I really do. Among the best I've met.'

< 2 >

'And it was like that all along the line,' he told Detective Superintendent Wiseman later that evening. 'Everyone I spoke to seemed to be tumbling over himself to give me detailed accounts of their movements that afternoon. They lunched at the hotel where they'd stayed when they arrived from Africa, so of course everyone there remembers them well, though not with unmitigated affection, I gather. They'd booked a table for one-thirty and turned up about ten minutes late and she even made a fuss because they hadn't been given her favourite table in the window. The head waiter tried to get it through to her that it was a table for four, but she got her own way in the end. I couldn't make out whether this was for the sake of peace, or whether Whitfield was doling out largesse in the background, but, anyway, they did themselves well and didn't leave the restaurant until well after three. The commissionaire remembers them too. They came out of the hotel ten or fifteen minutes later, but they didn't want him to call a taxi because they were going to walk through the Park, to work off some of their lunch. I don't know whether they did or not, but they set off in that direction and were inside the theatre an hour and a half later, so not even a helicopter could have got them

113

down here and back again in the time and that gets us nowhere.'

'You checked at the theatre, as well, did you?'

'Oh yes, and it was the same story there. It was the Criterion, by the way. I took a chance on it when I'd looked up the play and I went along and chatted up the people at the box office. It was most revealing.'

'But you didn't try your credit-card story on them?'

'No. Credit cards do play a part in it, but, if I'd used that dodge, they'd only have referred me to someone further up the line. But I had an idea that, if Christine and Whitfield had been there, the fact would have imprinted itself on the memory, in some way. So this time I was the poor wretch, up from the country, who'd been instructed by his partially blind and deaf aunt to get two tickets for the following week. They had to be in the front row of the dress circle, bang centre, that being the only position from which she could see and hear what was happening on stage. They couldn't oblige, of course. The play's a smash hit and they could practically sell every seat twice over. So I was very apologetic about my ignorance of the facts of London life and the box-office clerk took pity on me and said I wasn't the only one, by a long chalk. Just the other day there'd been a couple in, who'd booked by telephone, giving a credit-card number and, when they showed up to collect their tickets, the lady had practically gone through the roof and had held up the queue for about five minutes because they were in Row P, when she'd distinctly asked for Row E. She made a great scene about getting them changed and he had to explain that Row E was more expensive and, being a credit-card booking, there was damn all he could do about it. I made some joke about its being the sort of caper my elderly aunt went in for and he said that, whatever else, she wasn't anyone's elderly aunt. Not more than forty or so and quite a dasher, if you happened to like them red-haired and on the plump side. It all sounded conclusive enough to me, but you could always check with the credit-card company, if you needed proof.'

'What time was this? Five-ish?'

'Must have been. The curtain goes up at five-fifteen and they had to collect their tickets ten minutes in advance.'

'And how long does the performance run?'

'Two hours, twenty minutes, give or take.'

The Superintendent raised an eyebrow at this, but Frank shook his head.

'No. Sorry, sir, but that won't do, either. I agree that, with ten minutes' margin at each end, making a total of two hours, forty minutes, there might just have been time for one or both of them to get there and back in a fast car, but unfortunately we have to consider the interval.'

'You're not telling me they were seen together in the interval, too?'

'With bells on, I regret to say. They'd ordered drinks in advance. Nothing out of the way in that, but in this case it was champagne, which is sufficiently unusual to be remembered. What's more, after the final curtain they both made another visit to the bar. Normally, it would close down, after the interval, but of course on Saturdays they have an eight o'clock show to follow, so it stays open until nine-fifteen or nine-thirty.'

'More champagne?'

'No, it appears that she was wearing a silk dress with a matching jacket, and she'd taken the jacket off because it was so hot in the bar and then left it behind when they went back to their seats for the second half. All perfectly correct, as it turned out, and they'd kept it for her behind the bar.'

'So in other words, at approximately seven-fifteen they drove out of London and arrived at Beresford Court an hour and a quarter later, which, for a Saturday evening, is the average time it would have taken them. I call that sad, don't you?'

'Yes, sir, very.'

'On the other hand, do you get the feeling that it has all been laid on a trifle too thick?'

'In a sense, yes, I do, but I think there's another side to this particular coin. With most people, I grant you, such a display of personality in every chance encounter would appear unnatural, but I wouldn't be so sure about this one. I feel I've come to know her pretty well during the past twelve hours and I wouldn't be surprised if all this showing off was perfectly in line with her regular form. Her looks make her stand out, for a start. They all volunteered some remark about her colouring being so striking and she has a sort of bloom about her, which you don't often find in women of that age, unless they've been living outside the smog all their lives.'

'Yes, that struck me too.'

'Yes, you've met her, of course, sir, I was forgetting that. But wouldn't you also agree that she is someone who gets a great kick out of drawing attention to herself and does it almost automatically? They certainly seemed to take that view of her at the hotel; weren't remotely surprised when she demanded to have her table changed. You could tell it was the kind of thing that happened more often than not every time she went in there.'

'So you think we have to rule out those two entirely?'

'Well, it does begin to look like it, sir. I agree they were the obvious starting place, but, as far as that Saturday afternoon goes, we seem to be right up a gum tree. Whether the alibi was deliberately flaunted in our faces or not, I can't see a chance in the world of breaking it.'

'Although, when alibis are flaunted in faces, as you so graphically put it, one naturally tends to think that one's eye is being diverted deliberately.'

'Meaning that the staircase was damaged at some quite different time? But we've been through that, haven't we? Saturday afternoon and early evening would appear to be the only feasible period.'

'Yes, I'm afraid you're right, but, before we cast our theory to the winds, let's just have another look at Mr Jones's statement. You've got it there? Right. Now, first the telephone call on Sunday morning, when he claims to have spoken to both Mr and Mrs Marsh and a new time was set for the meeting at Bookers Farm.'

'Yes, here we are! The call came through at approximately ten o'clock. He was in his bedroom, so his daughter answered the phone and called him downstairs.'

'So no jiggery-pokery there, but I assume that we've checked that the call did come from the hotel?'

'Yes, we have. All outside calls have to go through the switchboard and a record is kept, so they can be charged on the weekly account. This one lasted in the region of ten minutes.'

'Which tallies with what Mr Jones told us. Where do we go next?'

'Well, we know that the appointment was put forward by one hour. There was quite a bit of argy-bargy about it because Mr Jones was reluctant to make it so late, whereas Mrs Marsh had wanted to postpone it even further; but then her husband came on the line and suggested

117

twelve-fifteen as a compromise, which is what they finally settled for.'

'Leaving a gap of approximately two hours between the telephone call and the meeting?'

'Well, not quite so much, actually. Allowing for the call having lasted ten minutes, plus the fact that Mr Jones claims to have arrived ten minutes ahead of time at the Farm and found Whitfield already there, it works out at nearer an hour and a half.'

'Right. And what do we know about the movements of all concerned during that period? Say, from ten-fifteen until eleven-forty-five?'

'Mr Jones says he was indoors, reading the Sunday papers. The other three were split up for most of the time. Mrs Marsh got the hotel porter to order a cab to take her to the hospital at eleven o'clock. She explained to him that her husband would be using their hired car to drive to church and she also mentioned that he and Whitfield would be able to collect her, so there would be no need for the driver to wait. She's very hot on saving the pennies, by all accounts. Marsh and Whitfield left the hotel together about half an hour before the taxi came for her.'

'And were they in church?'

'Well, that kind of thing is always rather tricky to establish, isn't it, sir? I mean, it's not as though you need a ticket to go in, or to bone up on the plot, or anything, but the indications are that they were there. The verger has to keep an eye on the cars, because it's a very narrow bit of lane up beside the church, where they're parked, and he's pretty certain he noticed one of Lubbock's cars. It's not much, but it all piles up. I presume you were thinking they might have gone straight to the farm?'

'There was that possibility, yes.'

'I know, but there's a major snag there too. Assuming Mr Jones's statement to be true, it was Marsh himself who fixed the new time and was unwilling to give up his church-going, so it doesn't seem likely that Whitfield could have persuaded him to do just that, in order to wait around in an empty, half-built house and watch him saw through a staircase, when he knew perfectly well that Mr Jones wouldn't turn up until more than an hour later.'

'What if Whitfield had dropped Marsh at the church, gone to the Farm and picked him up later?'

'That did occur to me, sir, but there are a couple of objections, I'm afraid. In the first place, the car which the verger thought he recognised as one of Lubbock's was pretty solidly wedged in between two others. Secondly, Mr Jones is quite positive that the main reason for their going to church at all was on Whitfield's account, so it's unlikely that he would then have consented to go on his own.'

'Assuming, as you say, Frank, that Mr Jones was telling us the truth.'

'Can you think of any reason why he shouldn't have done so?'

'Only one, as it happens; but, since Whitfield's statement concurs with his, in this respect, that would present us with a conspiracy of three, which is a bit too much to swallow.'

'Or a conspiracy of two, with Mrs Marsh as the innocent party?'

'Equally improbable, wouldn't you say? Well, it looks as though we'll have to pursue our second line of enquiry. I think I'd better handle that myself, but, in the mean time, Frank . . .'

'Sir?'

'Two little jobs for you. They're probably dead ends, but first I'd like you to check with Lubbock as to what each and every one of his cars and drivers was doing between midday on Saturday and midday on Sunday.'

'Very well, sir.'

'Your second task is not quite so humdrum and don't ask me how you're to go about it. I want you to find out a few details about an accident which occurred in Africa several months ago. I can't get them myself, because I have a feeling I may have blotted my copybook with those concerned, but I think you might have a shot.'

'What kind of accident would that be?' Frank asked, looking somewhat daunted.

'I've got the details written down here for you. It's a little matter of a murderous assault, which took place in or near the Marshes' tea estate.'

MONDAY, 20th AUGUST

The bricklayer who had been mainly responsible for the restoration of the seventeenth-century fireplace was putting the finishing touches to his work, which included polishing up the door of the little bread oven, when he made his great discovery.

Being also the man of whom Dolly had taken the diabolical liberty of accusing of the attempted theft of the fireback, he was naturally a trifle sensitive in this area and not above suspecting a deep-laid plot on her part to get him into further trouble. He therefore went at once to Cafferty and virtuously handed over his trophy, unopened and intact.

Cafferty was also making a great show of circumspection at this point and passed it on in the same state to Billy.

'How does he know it's only been there a few days?' Billy asked.

'Well, it's this way, d'you see. When he first had occasion to open the little oven he found it was choked solid with the soot of centuries, every ounce of it having to be removed before he could see how far the interior might be damaged. So it's hardly likely, you'll agree, Mr Jones, that, in transforming it to its present pristine state, the lad would have overlooked a parcel of even these dimensions.'

'No, I suppose not.'

'So it's my belief that we can dispense with any notions about its being part of the Crown Jewels looted by

Cromwell, for, seeing the box has no more than a speck of dust on it, it certainly hasn't been lying there for more than a week.'

'I am sure you are right,' Billy agreed, balancing the little square package on the palm of his hand. 'And, since Sir Robert is still the legal owner of Bookers, it would be fair to say that this is technically his property. He will have to decide what is best to be done about it.'

'Thank you very much, Mr Jones.'

'Not at all, Cafferty. Thank you.'

Billy was also being a little disingenuous, for nothing on earth would have induced him to approach Sir Robert in person, but the essence of what he said was true because he took the first opportunity to pay a call on Avril.

She not only agreed with him as to the probable nature of the contents of the package, but also had a theory to advance for its turning up in the bread oven.

'You can see at a glance that it's been opened and done up again. No self-respecting jeweller would have sent it out with that scruffy rubber band round it.'

'Perhaps not, but I don't see what that proves.'

'My dear Billy, use your loaf! Obviously, it fell out of the car when Martha was at Bookers that Saturday afternoon. One of the workmen must have found it among all that rubble they leave lying around in the yard, probably on Monday morning. Then, having seen what it contained, he popped it inside the oven for safe keeping.'

'Why would he do that, if he was intending to hang on to it? Why not just pop it inside his lunch-box?'

'Because, my dear oaf, the police were still on the premises and firing questions at everyone. Quite enough to put the wind up some of these scallywags. Our man may have imagined they were looking for this box, as part of the evidence, and if they didn't find it everyone would be searched, or something of that kind.'

'Yes, I suppose it's conceivable. But that was a week ago. The police haven't been near the place since the inquest. He's had plenty of opportunity to remove it in the mean time.'

'Ah well, that's where I may be one jump ahead of you. I should think he most likely has removed it.'

'What, and gone to all the trouble of tying up the box again and replacing it?'

'Odd, I grant you, but I dare say he had some reason at the back of his devious little mind.'

'Then hadn't we better open it and see if you're right? Not much point in chasing round to Martha and handing her an empty box.'

'Right, go ahead and open it.'

He did so, and inside, fitted snugly into its velvet lining, was an old-fashioned gold ring, set with a garnet, surrounded by pearls.

'Well, what do you know?' Avril said. 'I apologise to him, whoever he is. It's either some absent-minded squirrel type, who hides things and forgets where he put them, or else there is some entirely different explanation for this mystery. I confess I feel curious.'

'Real stones, would you say?'

'No question at all. Victorian, most likely, and it must have cost a veritable bomb. Pretty too, isn't it? I should think Martha will be pleased. You'd better ring her right away and warn her to get out the sal volatile.'

'You don't think we ought to mention it to Tubby first?'

'Certainly not. Nothing whatever to do with him. It may be stolen property, in a sense, but she's got it back now and, in any case, its loss was never reported. Martha didn't even try to claim the insurance.'

'All the same, don't you think . . . ?'

'What? What are you on about, Billy?'

'That there's the barest possibility that it could be tied up with Marsh's death, in some way?'

'Ah! Well, I admit that hadn't occurred to me. How could it be, though?'

Billy shook his head. 'Oh, God knows. Purest coincidence, I expect, but it simply struck me as faintly sinister that it should have turned up where it did.'

'Yes, you may well have something there. I tell you what I think we should do. Hand it over to Martha forthwith, before anything else happens to it, and ask her if she has any objection to our passing the news on to Tubby. He's dining here tonight, as it happens, and I'd be fascinated to know what construction he puts on it, but get her permission first. If she prefers to keep it dark, I won't breathe a word.'

'All right, I'll call in on my way home and find out how she feels about it.'

He was as good as his word and less than an hour later telephoned to report that Martha was speechless with shock and surprise, but had nodded assent to the suggestion of Tubby's being informed.

< 2 >

Adrian and Miranda had been less fortunate, for their enterprise had been designed to yield up a treasure and did not.

Miranda had remained in the driving seat, with the engine running and a sardonic expression on her face, as she watched Adrian swagger up to the entrance of

124

the Beresford Court Hotel, then pause on the top step to square his puny shoulders, before disappearing into the foyer. As soon as he had vanished she had switched off the engine, because she deplored waste and estimated that she would have ample time to get the motor running again when he reappeared on the steps, weighed down by his prize.

However, when he emerged about fifteen minutes later he was empty-handed and it was evident from his furious, pinched little face, and from the force with which he slammed the car door shut, that the expedition had been a complete rout.

'What happened?'

'Get going, for God's sake,' he snarled, brushing the back of his hand across his eyes.

'Okay, but what's the hurry, since it turns out you're not a criminal on the run, after all?'

'I'd just like to get away from this rotten dump, if you don't mind.'

'What happened, then?' she asked again when they were on the road. 'Wouldn't they let you have the key?'

'Oh, they gave me the key all right, no trouble at all. The only slight disadvantage was,' he said with heavy sarcasm, 'that when I got to her room the thing wasn't there.'

'Oh, bad luck! Flogged it already, has she?'

'No, I wish she had, in a way, because I might have been able to find out who to and somehow got hold of the money to buy it back again. It wouldn't cost so much second-hand.'

'What's she done with it, then?'

'When I couldn't find it in her room I thought at first she might have given it to Dad to look after. I was rather bucked because that would have made things a whole lot easier, in a way. So I went downstairs to ask for his key

125

and the fool of a woman at the desk asked me why I
wanted it.'

'Did you tell her?'

'Had to, didn't I? And you know what? Mum's had it
put in the hotel safe and they're not allowed to take anything out of there without her written permission. Can you
beat that? Tapes, compact discs, the lot! She's had them
all carted away and locked in the bloody, stinking safe.'

'Well, I never!'

'Is that all you can say?'

'No, I could say a lot, but there doesn't seem much
point.'

'Oh, doesn't there? Well, I'm not so easily put off, I'd
like you to know. I thought everything would get better,
now my stepfather's dead, but this is worse than anything.
It's downright stealing, that's what, and I'm damn well
going to do something about it. Just you wait and see!'

'Mind you, I think we'll have to wait a long time,' Miranda
told her father that evening, 'because, as far as I can see,
she's got him by the short hairs.'

She was sitting cross-legged on the floor of Billy's
studio, practising her yoga exercises, while he attempted,
without much success, to resuscitate some enthusiasm for
the Parish Council's cricket pavilion.

'Of course, I wouldn't have been spilling all these
beans, if he had pulled it off,' she went on. 'I have a
very strict code about that sort of thing, and there was
also the fact that the less you knew about it the better.
But since it was such a total flop there doesn't seem
much harm in telling you. Always assuming that you're
listening.'

'Oh, I am, I am.'

'The woman sounds a complete virago.'

'She may have her reasons. You have only heard one side of the story.'

'Oh yes, you would stick up for her! I expected that.'

'Did you? Why?' he asked, briefly opening his eyes and adding a little shading to his pretty, domed roof.

'Because everyone knows you had the most ghastly crush on her when you were young.'

'Who told you that?'

'Millions of people. It's a well-known fact that you wanted to marry her. Thank God someone else cut you out, is all I can say.'

'Two other people cut me out, as it happens.'

'And bully for them! I only hope that meeting her again in your dotage hasn't revived all the old passions.'

'No, it hasn't.'

'In view of her current situation, I'm mighty relieved to hear it.'

'Listen, Miranda,' Billy said, laying down his pencil and glancing at her in a speculative way. 'Perhaps it is time that you and I had a little chat. I realise that I have not been a model father, in every respect, but surely I cannot have neglected to tell you that your mother and I have never been divorced? Even if Christine were a widow, twice over, which she is not, there really wouldn't be the slightest danger of your getting her as your stepmother.'

'Oh, I know that,' she replied cheerfully. 'I didn't imagine that even you would be barmy enough to want to marry her. That wasn't what worried me.'

'No? What, then?'

'Well, you see, Pa, if it got around that you were still stuck on her, people might get the wrong idea about a certain event.'

'What event would that be?' he asked, swivelling away from her and taking up his pencil again.

'The one in which Adrian's stepfather took a toss down the stairs. Looking at it dispassionately, it seems to me that you had the best opportunity of anyone for applying the fatal shove. If I can see it, the chances are that other people can too, and it would be rather a shame if they could link it up with a tiny motive.'

'I am grateful to you for pointing it out,' Billy said civilly, 'and let us hope it has cleared the air. You need worry yourself no further. I am not cut out for the *crime passionnel*, as anyone who knows me will confirm. My own well-being is my principal pre-occupation these days, apart from yourself, I need hardly add, and there is something else you have overlooked.'

'What's that?'

'That I had more to lose than most people by the poor fellow's death. If I were going to knock him off, you may be sure I would have waited until the house was finished and my fee had been paid.'

'True, very true,' Miranda agreed. 'If anyone starts anything, I'll mention that. Which reminds me, have you got any money on you at this moment?'

'What sort of money?'

'Oh, just a fiver, or so. I'm right out and our poor little deprived guest is in a black humour this evening. I thought of taking him to the movies.'

'Oh, in that case,' Billy said, turning out his pockets, 'you are more than welcome. Take whatever you need.'

When she had gone he climbed down from his stool and picked up the photograph album, which was still lying on the floor where he had left it. It fell open at the page he had been studying before, but this time it was not the snapshot which interested him, but information of a different kind, and he was gratified to discover that his memory had not let him down. In the centre of the page and symmetrically ringed by five surrounding photographs, these words were inscribed in his own italic script: *Paris, August 5th.*

He closed the album again and dropped it back on the floor. He believed there was little chance of anyone else showing any curiosity in it, still less of their drawing relevant conclusions, and he wanted it to remain accessible. It was true, as he had assured Miranda, that his heart no longer lay at Christine's feet, but enough of the old feeling remained to make him hesitate to throw her to the wolves. On the whole, he was confident that he would do so only if his own position were to be endangered. In the interests of both of them, therefore, it was essential to work out a formula for self-protection and, as a preliminary step, he picked up his pencil again and began an exercise in forgery.

< 3 >

Telephoning in his report, Frank caught Tubby at a moment when he was dressing to go to dinner with Avril and was therefore advised to make it snappy.

'Just to let you know, sir, that, so far as it goes, Lubbock has a clean record for the whole of Saturday and Sunday.'

'I thought he probably would, but what do you mean by "so far as it goes"?'

'Well, you know Lubbock, sir. Always willing to lose his memory to satisfy a good customer, and even in these inflationary days a tenner or two doesn't come amiss.'

'Yes, thank you, Frank, I did know that. What about the other business?'

'Wheels in motion, sir. I'll keep you informed.'

'Well done, my boy. That all?'

'That's all for the present, sir.'

'Well, thank you, Frank. Goodnight and bon appetit.'

'Thank you, sir, and the same to you.'

FRIDAY, 24th AUGUST

Their recent disastrous encounter had naturally tended to make Christine wary of strangers, and Tim even more so, but when she received a letter from Sir Arthur Brown, written from his home near Sevenoaks, it did not occur to her to question its authenticity, any more than its sincerity.

Sir Arthur had been the last Governor-General of the territory in East Africa where Christine had spent so many years of her life, and which had been the swan-song of his long and distinguished career. She had met him only twice, when she was very young, but he and Lady Brown had once visited the Marshes' estate, when Derek's father had arranged a safari trip for them, and, although this was in the days when she was the newly married Mrs Whitfield, she had been invited to the dinner party which had been given in his honour.

She had taken particular pains with her appearance on that occasion and exerted her charm and vivacity to the utmost, but, although there was hardly another man present who could take his eyes off her, H.E. had seemed far more interested in talking about bygone days with Derek's dreary old mother. She had been obliged to write him off as one of her few failures and was therefore all the more gratified to discover how deep was the impression she had made. For why else would he have taken the trouble to write to her so charmingly to condole on her tragic loss?

It was true, as it turned out, that this was not the sole purpose of his letter, but the secondary motive was equally flattering in its way.

Having expounded on Derek's virtues in two paragraphs, with passing references to the splendid contribution which he and his family had made to the development of their adopted country, Sir Arthur wrote as follows:

You will perhaps find it insensitive of me to touch on another matter at this sad time and, if so, please disregard what I am about to ask of you now. I shall understand perfectly, but my difficulty is that when it first became known to me that you and Derek were back in this country, I was asked to approach you on behalf of my young godson and, having promised to do so, found myself putting it off from day to day, as one is unhappily all too prone to do at my age. However, the point has now arrived where the subject must be broached at once, or not at all, and I therefore crave your forbearance.

The young man (his name is Frank Armstrong, by the way) has recently joined one of the United Nations agencies and has been posted to Ngudu which, if memory serves, is pretty much in your territory, where he is to be in charge of an ambitious agricultural project. If you meet him, he will be able to give you the details far better than I can, but I do know that the job will involve recruiting a sizeable team of Africans for training and to work alongside him. Since he has never set foot in that part of the world, you may well think him an odd choice for the job (but ours not to reason why) and, to give him his due, he is quite properly a little apprehensive about the prospect and anxious to arm himself with as much foreknowledge as possible. I, alas, am sadly out of date on conditions there now and can only give him the scantiest of practical advice. He could no doubt get plenty of information from those of his countrymen who are still on the spot, including our High Commissioner, who is an old friend, but I understand there is a danger for members of the UN in being seen to have national affiliations and Frank is anxious to avoid this pitfall as far as possible.

Faced with this dilemma, who better than your-self, so recently returned, so close to government circles and, above all, with such vast experience of the territory and its people, to solve it for us? I should take it very kindly if you would consent to see him and to 'put him in the picture', as they say nowadays, and I must repeat that I can only hope that you will not regard this as too great an impor-tunity. Perhaps you agree with me that we want our young men to acquit themselves as creditably under the new flag as their fathers did under the old and, if so, I hope to receive a line from you, giving per-mission for Frank to make himself known to you. He is due to leave these shores at the end of next week.

                    With kindest regards, Yours, etc. . . .

She lost no time in responding to this civil request, couch-ing her permission in cordial, yet dignified terms, and two days later Frank Armstrong telephoned to ask if he might call on her. She invited him to tea on the following Sunday, which did not please his wife very much, for the lawn was in urgent need of attention, but, since the choice of time and date had been left entirely to Christine, there was no backing out.

< 2 >

Structural work on the house was nearing completion and Billy's worries kept pace with it. Several members of the work crew, which he and the building firm had assembled with such difficulty at very short notice, were already idle, owing to Christine's inability or unwillingness to make up her mind about the fittings for the kitchen and bathrooms, the style of built-in cupboards for the bedrooms and the wallpaper and paint throughout. So, while costs continued to rocket, there was less and less to show for them.

Most of his anxiety was on Avril's behalf, for at this stage Robert was still footing the bills and his profit on the sale, which had been marginal in the first place, was rapidly dwindling away to the point where it would turn into a loss.

She advised him to let things ride for another week, to give Christine time to sort out her financial position, but he considered that even this was stretching it too far, as there was now an hourly risk of some of the work force being called off to other jobs.

'What do you suggest, then?' Avril asked.

'I think we must try to have a proper meeting and get it thrashed out, once and for all. I've made one or two attempts to get some sense out of her on the telephone, but as soon as we get anywhere near brass tacks she starts crying and accusing me of browbeating her. I think the only solution is to invite her and Tim to lunch or dinner one day, and I'd like you to be there too, if you will. I shall need your moral support and I have a feeling that she won't go in so much for the weepy stunt in your presence.'

'I'll do better than that, Billy boy, I'll invite them to dinner here. It will be more suitable than your house because it has no associations with Derek. Besides, unfamiliar surroundings often have an inhibiting effect on the tear ducts. Get yourself a drink while I go and ring her up.'

This was highly satisfactory and, while she was out of the room, he also helped himself to two or three sheets of her writing paper and slipped them into his brief-case. In a few minutes she was back, to report that the invitation had been extended for Sunday evening and accepted on the nail. Whereupon, he took his leave and hurried home to begin an afternoon's solid work.

It began with a search through the file labelled 'Bookers Farm', which, in addition to copies of estimates and schedules, contained an assortment of correspondence, including a letter which Christine had written to him from London, stipulating the addition of the extra bathroom, and it ended with his going in search of Miranda.

'I shall be out to dinner on Sunday,' he informed her, 'and I am going to ask Martha if she will have Adrian. This will give you a free evening.'

'Thanks very much. Why do I need a free evening?'

'Because there is a little task I wish you to perform for me and I consider it preferable that Adrian should not be a witness.'

'I can't wait to hear.'

'I shall want you to drive me to Avril's dinner party and then bring the car back here. At some time between eight-thirty and nine, I should like you to set forth again and deliver this letter to the Beresford Court Hotel. It is, as you see, addressed to the Manager and I would prefer you to hand it to him personally, since he is unlikely to be on the scene when you make your second visit, which I will come to in a minute. This will reduce the chances of his remembering the incident. However, if he is not

135

available, you will just have to use your own judgment.'

'Gladly. Will there be an answer?'

'I sincerely hope so, and if there is, you will need both hands to carry it. However, there is no necessity for you to collect me from Avril's party. Christine and Tim will be there and they can give me a lift.'

'Well, honestly, Pa, you amaze me! It's not like you to exert yourself to gratify the whim of a spotty youth.'

Billy shook his head. 'No, that is not the object, which is partly why I have decided that it would be wiser for Adrian to be kept in the dark. We shall not be keeping these articles, you understand, just borrowing them for a few hours. Early on Monday morning, with your co-operation, they will all be returned. Or nearly all,' he added thoughtfully. 'Now, pay attention, Miranda, while I outline the rest of the programme. It is a matter of some gravity and I cannot afford the slightest hitch.'

'Rely on me,' Miranda told him. 'I shall enjoy putting a spoke in the virago's wheel.'

SUNDAY, 26th AUGUST

Avril's dinner party was a huge success and they even suc-
ceeded in making some headway in the business for which
it had been convened. Christine had had another long talk
with Charles Lawson, who had urged her to press on with
the exchange of contracts, since she could just squeeze out
enough money and, as she naïvely remarked, he was of
the opinion that it would prove to be a better investment
than most.

She was looking ethereally beautiful in her new black
jersey silk dress and was noticeably subdued and sorrow-
ful, to begin with, but soon warmed up during dinner and
became quite animated after her second glass of burgundy.
By degrees, it emerged that it was not solely the heartening
advice she had received from Charles Lawson which had
put new life into her; there was also the exceedingly
pleasant afternoon she had just spent with one Frank
Armstrong, the protégé of her dear old friend, Sir Arthur
Brown. Avril nearly fell out of her chair on hearing this,
but she covered up by pretending that it was Sir Arthur's
name which was familiar. She became rather vague as to
where they had met, or how long ago, but soon managed
to extricate herself from the difficulty by encouraging
Christine to tell them more about the charming godson,
which drew a lengthy and detailed response.

Tim grew perceptibly more morose as the evening wore
on, but otherwise all went as merry as a marriage bell,

and Miranda also carried out her end of the business in exemplary fashion. When Billy returned home just before midnight, he found a note on the hall table, which read as follows:

Mission accomplished. A. is spending the night with Martha. She will telephone in the morning to explain, but no cause for alarm. Sleep well. M.

He repaired to his studio and spent a profitable and instructive hour and a half there, before crawling upstairs to bed.

< 2 >

By a curious coincidence, Frank had also been enjoying some fine burgundy, while dining with his Chief and giving his own version of the afternoon's events.

'It wasn't all plain sailing at first,' he had begun by explaining, 'because Whitfield was hanging around when I got there, obviously with every intention of muscling in on the tea party, and I remembered your warning me that he was the more cagey of the two. So I had to spend about twenty minutes trying to choke him off with my long and tedious descriptions of the United Nations agricultural policies. It was touch and go, as a matter of fact, because she was getting almost as bored as he was, but luckily he cracked first and went off to write some letters, or something. I forget the exact excuse.'

'And after that?'

'Oh, after that it went like a bomb. She's inclined to be susceptible to flattery and not quite so self-assured as she appears on the surface. She feels on safer ground when she's harking back to the old days in Africa, and once she gets started on that, there's practically no holding her. It's a bit like taking money out of the blind man's hat.'

'Which didn't deter you, I trust?'

'No, although I can't take much credit for that because she made it all so dead easy. We got on to the subject of the murderous assault almost without any prodding at all, though, mind you, she claimed to be telling me about it simply as a warning not to trust anyone. However loyal and friendly they might appear to be one day, they wouldn't hesitate to carve you up with a hatchet the next, and so on and so on.'

'Is that literally what happened?'

'More or less. It was the kind of incident one hears about from that part of the world from time to time, though in this case not fatal, as you know. What upset her most was that one of their own servants was the culprit; not a labourer on the estate, but what she described as a house-boy. He'd been with the family for twenty years, what's more. It was that incident which finally decided them to pack it in and seek the safety of Sussex.'

'Yes, Miss Kershaw mentioned something about it a month or so ago, but she hadn't heard the details. Where did the attack take place? In the house?'

'No, at the office. The house is some distance away from the estate, but the office building is slap in the middle of it. Marsh and Whitfield each had a room on the first floor and the incident occurred at around seven in the evening, when the clerical staff had left. That means, in effect, that it could have been aimed at either one of them, or, conceivably, both.'

'How do you make that out?'

'Because of the work routine. I should explain that

139

there's hardly any variation in the length of the days out there. It's practically on the equator, so the same pattern is followed throughout the year. The office staff worked in the usual way, from nine till five, but the plantation people had a different system. The first shift came on at seven in the morning and the second shift went off at seven at night. There was also a third system, which applied only to the management, in other words, Marsh and Whitfield.'

'And what did they do?'

'They clocked in at seven a.m., come rain come shine, went home to lunch and took the rest of the afternoon off, for siestas, or tennis, or whatever; then one or other of them, occasionally both, would go back just before five to clear up odds and ends and remain there until every last man was off the premises and the night watch came on. On the evening in question they were both there.'

'The evening when Marsh was attacked?'

'When Whitfield was attacked, sir.'

'Are you sure?'

'Oh yes, positive. What happened was that Whitfield had been out of doors to raise some query with one of the overseers and, when he came in, it was just beginning to get dark. So he switched on the lights and saw some chap creeping upstairs, with a whacking great pickaxe in his hand. It was one of the local tools, which they all use, even to this day, for turning over the soil, but of course there could only have been one reason for this chap to be carrying it at such a time, or for being inside the building at all, come to that. Anyway, Whitfield made a dash for him and this African lashed out and struck him a terrific blow on the arm, which pretty well knocked him out. Whereupon Joshua, that was his name by the way, made a dash for it. Whitfield was too shattered to go after him and the theory is that he must have mingled with the afternoon shift, who were just knocking off, and then run the couple of hundred miles back to his own village. It seems that, when they do that, you have about as much chance of catching up with them as of finding one individual tree in the forest.'

'Well, congratulations, my dear boy. By and large, you've done very well.'

'I hope it's told you what you wanted to know.'

'I shouldn't be surprised. No direct bearing on what happened here, of course. Possibly no connection of any kind, but it never hurts to fill in some of the background. And now you must be quite dry after all that talking, so let me give you a glass of port. It's a rather special one my wine merchant put me on to the other day and I'll give you a quid if you can get within ten years of its date.'

< 3 >

A less convivial, but far more sensational evening had just ended for Martha Kershaw, in which the mystery surrounding Derek's present had taken an unnerving step towards clarification.

She had not dared to wear the ring in Dolly's presence, shirking the endless tedium which would be involved in explaining how she had come by it and the inevitable jealous tantrums which would follow. But Dolly, who did not much care for Adrian, had opted for supper in bed when she learned that he was expected. Having taken up her tray and placed the materials for a letter to Alice Barnby close at hand, Martha repaired to her own room, to change out of her gardening trousers into a clean dress. It was an occasion, of a sort, for she did not often have visitors in the evening, and she had laid in a bottle of cider and arranged her menus around pork chops and fried potatoes, followed by lemon sorbet, which were Adrian's favourites. The garnet and pearl ring added the final gala touch.

All the same, she had to take it off again to peel the potatoes and she hung it on a spare cup-hook. Whereupon, being unaccustomed to wearing jewellery at any time, as well as extremely feckless about personal possessions, she promptly forgot all about it.

Adrian gobbled up every mouthful that was put in front of him, but in other respects was a disappointing guest, being sunk in the deepest mire of self-pity and sulks and requiring her to fight every inch of the way to get a monosyllabic response. It occurred to her that Billy might just possibly have some justification for the broad hints he had been dropping that Adrian was suffering from pangs of love for Miranda and therefore resented being forced to spend an evening away from her. So she attempted to draw him out by saying what an attractive girl Miranda was and how much he must enjoy having a companion of his own generation, all of which he furiously denied and then became more surly than ever.

In desperation, she suggested a game of chess and, for the first time, a spark of enthusiasm enlivened his features. Encouraged by this, Martha silently vowed that, whatever his standard of play, on this occasion he should be the winner.

The only suitable table was the one in the dining room, so she asked him to help her clear away the supper and then put the kettle on for coffee, while she looked for the chess-board. This took longer than she had expected, since she had not had an opportunity to bring it out for several years and, when she returned to the kitchen, she was horrified to find Adrian leaning over the sink, apparently in a gastric convulsion. His colour had turned so ashen

142

that the pimples stood out on his forehead like a regiment of red dots.

'Adrian, my dear, what on earth's the matter?'

'Nothing,' he replied in a choked voice. 'I feel sick, that's all.'

He then pushed his way past her and tore upstairs to the bathroom.

There followed a nerve-racking period in which, between pounding on the bathroom door with anxious enquiries to Adrian and trying to silence the screams of curiosity which poured from Dolly's room, Martha herself was torn by doubts as to the quality of the pork chops.

'But I don't see how it can have been the pork,' she muttered, wringing her hands, as he emerged at last. 'It wouldn't have come on so soon. How are you feeling now?'

'Better,' he mumbled. 'Can I go home now? I mean, where I'm staying?'

He had regained some of his colour, but still looked wretchedly ill and it was evident that he had been crying, so she asked, 'Will there be anyone there? I know Billy was going out to dinner, but what about Miranda?'

'I don't know.'

'Then try and think, there's a good boy. Or perhaps I had better ring up and see?'

'She said something about going out too,' he admitted, staring down at his feet. 'That's why I was supposed to come here.'

'Then I honestly think you'll have to spend the night, Adrian. Yes, my dear, I insist. You don't look at all well and you might easily have another attack. It's not as though I could stay with you until one of them gets back. The best I could do would be to drop you off there and then come haring back, because of leaving Granny.'

To her immense relief, he did not argue, for once, but stood limply by while she struggled with the camp-bed. When it was all in place, she went to the kitchen to fetch him a glass of water, a plastic bowl and a towel, which she placed on the floor by the bed. He was already buried under the covers when she returned, with only a patch of red-gold hair visible, and she addressed herself to this, as she picked up his jeans and shirt from the floor and hung them over the back of a chair.

'I'll be close at hand in the kitchen for an hour or so and I'll leave my door open when I go up, so just call out if you need anything.'

He did not reply and ten minutes later, when she crept back to the dining room, it was apparent from his breathing that he had fallen asleep.

By a logical association of ideas, it was while she was washing up the wire chip-basket that she finally remembered her ring and went over to the shelf where she had left it. There was one empty hook in the middle of the row, but this was accounted for by the presence of a coffee cup, which had been left lying on its side on the table underneath. Three hooks further along the ring still hung exactly as she had left it.

MONDAY, 27th AUGUST

'Yes, naturally, I'm worried,' Martha confessed the following morning. 'Who wouldn't be? The implications are far too serious and I don't see how they can be ignored.'

She had left the house as soon as Mrs Bailey had got her coat off and received her instructions, which included not disturbing the occupant of the dining room, and had driven straight to Avril's house for a consultation. She had found her in the dining room, sharing her hearty breakfast with her bulldog and Pekinese, who were named Blanche and Tray, Sweet having been run over six months previously.

'What have you done with the ring now?' Avril enquired. 'Locked it up in a safe place, I trust?'

'Oh yes, I wouldn't be so careless with it a third time. Not that I believe there's much danger of his taking it again. The mere sight of it last night obviously filled him with such terror and revulsion that he became physically ill.'

'Well, you've got it back, that's the main thing, and you always said he was a deceitful little lad, so you won't die of disillusionment.'

'Yes, but thieving, Avril! I never dreamt he was capable of that.'

'I know, and I do wonder why he did it and then hid it in such an extraordinary place. Do you suppose he's just a natural delinquent, or is it some frightful Freudian thing, like compensating for his ghastly parents' neglect?'

Martha shook her head. 'I fear not. I'd like to believe it was something of that kind, but I'm afraid there was a purely practical incentive. I came across a half-written letter of his, when I was packing up his suitcase to send over to Billy's. I know I ought not to have read it, but it was lying face upward and it was rather too much to resist. I wish I hadn't now and I wish, most of all, that we hadn't told Tubby about the ring being lost and found again. Also, I don't agree with you about the oven being an extraordinary hiding place. Given his limited resources, I consider it was rather imaginative.'

'So what comes next? Do you confront him with it?'

'I honestly don't know. I've been lying awake half the night worrying about it. That's why I'm here. I thought you might be able to give me some advice.'

'Well, as you know, I'm always ready with that,' Avril admitted, 'and my advice is to have it out with him. You could be mistaken, you know, and it will at least clear the air.'

Martha shuddered. 'Will it? I strongly doubt that. I think he would most likely deny it flatly and we should be worse off than ever. I shouldn't know any more than I do now and I'd have to put up with a lot more hostility than I'm getting already. If only I liked him better, it would be easier,' she added mournfully, 'but, try as I may, I just don't seem able to work up much affection for him.'

'Poor Martha!' Avril said sympathetically. 'You do have a hard time, don't you? I never knew anyone with such a repulsive set of relations.'

'And that's not the worst of it, I might tell you. There's also the fact that if, by some miracle, he were to own up to having stolen the beastly thing, we'd still be stuck with all those implications I mentioned just now.'

'Oh, would we? I thought we'd covered the implications?'

'Far from it. The situation is much graver than you seem to realise.'

'Then put me straight, please.'

'Well, we know, don't we, that the ring must have been taken from my car at some time on that Saturday afternoon or early evening?'

'Yes, I suppose we do.'

'Now, assuming that Adrian did take it, when is the only possible time he could have transferred it to Bookers and deposited it in the oven? That's to say, between Saturday evening and Derek's arrival there on Sunday morning?'

'Are you asking me, or telling me?'

'I'm terribly afraid I'm telling you because, whichever way you look at it, by my reckoning the only time would have been very early on Sunday morning, before Derek got there and went into the house on his own.'

'Now, Martha dearest, do take a pull! You can't seriously be suggesting that Adrian was inside the house when his step-father arrived and that he pushed him downstairs, having first had the forethought to make a large enough hole?'

'That wouldn't necessarily follow. He might have found the large hole already there, and perhaps that gave him the idea.'

'But all the same.'

'I know, I know. It's too dreadful to contemplate, I agree, but it's been preying on my mind all night and I simply have to confide in someone. You see, however fantastic, it's not utterly impossible. He really did loathe Derek and he was under this pathetic illusion that his

147

mother would be a different person, if he could be got rid of.'

'Then I can only imagine he must have been badly disappointed. But, honestly, Martha, I do think you're barking up the wrong tree this time. I can't believe even that unattractive child would be capable of such a thing.'

'He's not really a child, you know. He's seventeen and they've been known to commit violent crimes at that age.'

'He may not be a child, but he still has the physique of one. When you consider their respective sizes, you must see that Adrian simply wouldn't have had the physical strength for it.'

'Would it have needed much strength, though? In the dark and with Derek probably flailing about like some wretched hippopotamus? Surely the merest nudge would have tipped him off balance?'

'Well, I don't know, Martha. You make it sound plausible, in a way, but I have to admit I'm properly stumped this time.'

'But what do you think I should do?'

'Nothing, for the time being, obviously. We'll have to tread warily here. I'm thinking of you, principally. If your theory is right, it's your evidence which is going to put him away for ten or twelve years. That won't be much fun for you.'

'No, it won't,' Martha agreed, sounding positively relieved, 'and I'm grateful to you for pointing it out. That was one implication which I'd overlooked. So it seems I shall just have to try and put the whole business out of my mind.'

'Well, perhaps not right out,' Avril remarked thoughtfully. 'It may not be in the best interests of the public safety that he should be running around like some dear little Orestes on the loose. He might try his luck with you or Billy next, if one of you said anything to annoy him.'

'So what's the alternative?'

'I'm not sure, but I think we should try to find a way of getting to the truth, without bringing you into it at all. Perhaps I might drop a hint to Tubby?'

'Wouldn't that amount to the same thing? He'd be sure to start by asking where you got your information.'

'I wouldn't be compelled to tell him. But still, you're probably right,' Avril said, buttering a piece of toast and handing it to Tray. 'He's a clever Dick, when it comes to getting blood out of a stone. You'd better give me time to think it over. I've seen quite a lot of nasty little boys and girls passing through the Juvenile Court in my time and, if I concentrate, I may get a clue about what action to take. Just lie low and leave it with me for a day or two.'

It was not Martha's idea of a perfect solution, but at least it had removed part of the burden from her own shoulders, and she drove home in a slightly calmer frame of mind than she had started out with.

< 2 >

In devising his elaborate plot for pulling the carpet from under Christine's feet, Billy had overlooked two important contingencies. One of them was out of his control, but the other could easily have been foreseen.

The area of ignorance derived from the fact that, in telling Adrian that the recording machinery was locked in the hotel safe, the receptionist had been employing a euphemism. The truth was that it was far too bulky for the safe, which was not normally required to house anything larger than a tiara, and for this reason the Manager had consented to keep it in a cupboard in his office, the key of which was on his own personal ring. Therefore, when Miranda handed back all but one of the borrowed articles early on Monday morning, they were not, as Billy had hopefully envisaged, returned to the safe before the Manager was up and about his business and as promptly forgotten. Instead, they were placed on a table in his office, for him to deal with when he chose. By an added stroke of bad luck, he had only just tucked them back in the cupboard when he met Christine in the foyer and took it upon himself to assure her that her valuables had been returned and were once more under lock and key.

He might have thought twice about doing so if he had known that this news, when amplified and explained, would send her into flaming hysterics, but that, in fact, is what happened.

When she had been quietened down and escorted to her bedroom, she refused to allow a doctor to be called, blaming the outburst on her recent tragic loss and, although still pale and trembling, put the Manager through a full and detailed interrogation of the events leading up to his disclosure. Enquiries were then put on foot among other members of the staff and, although none of those on duty at the time of Miranda's two visits had recognised her, neither Christine nor Tim had the slightest difficulty in doing so from their descriptions.

At the end of all this Christine announced that she would take a sedative and did not wish to be disturbed and, in fact, the Do Not Disturb notice was not taken down for the rest of that morning. Christine spent the time alternately moaning and wringing her hands and rounding on Tim with furious reproaches for allowing such a thing to happen to her. It was not until lunch time that she grew calm enough to consider some counter-measures, and when these were completed they took a very different form from any that Billy had allowed for.

What he had realised all along was that if, despite his precautions, she came to hear about the temporary theft, she would instantly recognise the cause and effect, including the probability of one item not having been returned, and indeed a count of them had been among the first of her demands. What had not entered into his calculations was the fact that she would unquestioningly assume Miranda to have been the moving spirit in the affair, although acting with the knowledge and connivance of Adrian.

She did not stop to ask herself what could have induced Miranda to behave in such a fashion, nor how she had acquired a supply of Avril's writing paper. She did not even pause to reflect that it was curious that Miranda could have achieved such a perfect copy of another woman's handwriting, despite the fact that, when first shown the letter, she actually had the greatest difficulty in believing that she had not written it herself. Her one and only thought was to find a way to trick Miranda into parting with her prize, so that it might be finally and forever destroyed, which she was now inclined to reprimand Tim for not having done in the first place.

'Not so blinking easy,' he pointed out. 'Couldn't very well chuck it in the waste-paper basket. No telling where it might have landed up. Straight into that Superintendent's lap, for all we know.'

'But still, there must have been other ways.'

'I don't know what they are. It would probably have gummed up the works, if I'd shoved it down the loo. I doubt if it would have burnt, even if I'd managed to sneak out to the incinerator, and we haven't got a lake handy. Besides, we both agreed it was safe where it was.'

'I know, and look how wrong we were! Oh, I could murder that girl, I really could. No, I don't mean that,' she amended hastily, 'but I've got to think of some way of forcing her to give it back. You'd better go down and have a drink and leave me to work something out.'

'Righty-ho!' he said, moving off with such alacrity that he was halfway through the door before she managed to deliver her final warning.

'And, for God's sake, be careful, Tim. Don't go yapping to every Tom, Dick and Harry who buys you a pint of beer.'

'Count on me, old girl,' he said, and shut the door firmly behind him.

Christine sat down at her dressing table and stared at her reflection in the glass. It was a sight which had often been known to restore confidence and bring solace to a troubled mind and it did not let her down on this occasion. She was very soon able to marshal her thoughts and hit on a plan to confound the enemy.

The completed formula, had she but known it, contained certain similarities to the one which Billy had invented for her, since it began by her inviting him to lunch.

Probably he should have known better and been on his guard, for, in her present straitened circumstances, the offer of a cup of tea or, at the very most, a gin and tonic would have been more in character. However, he rashly concluded that, having uncovered the trick that had been played on her and having also tumbled to his part in it, she intended to launch her counter-attack by softening him up with the best that the Beresford Court kitchens could provide. He was also distinctly curious to learn how it would develop from that point.

Unfortunately, nothing was to turn out at all as he had anticipated.

< 3 >

Frank, it transpired, had also taken too much for granted and, among several misapprehensions, was his belief that he was to have Monday morning off.

'Your Chief telephoned,' his wife informed him, when he made a late appearance, dressed in his lawn-mowing clothes. 'He said I needn't bother to wake you up and he asked me to give you a message.'

'Then please break it gently,' he pleaded.

'He said it might be worth your while to pay another visit to the theatre.'

'Why? I thought I'd covered that pretty exhaustively already.'

'Yes, but he said you shouldn't bother with the box office this time. Concentrate on the barmaid who served the champagne.'

'In God's name, what's he after now? Does he want to know the vintage, or something?'

'No, I've got it all written down for you. Pour yourself some coffee while I read it out.'

It was a comparatively long message, and while he was listening to it Frank sat with his jaw cupped in his hands, staring at the wall opposite him, as though debating whether to get up and start knocking his head against it.

TUESDAY, 28th AUGUST

Martha's first act on returning from her early morning call
on Avril was to tiptoe into the dining room, to see how
Adrian was getting on. He was awake, but looked distress-
ingly flushed and hollow-eyed. She took his temperature
and was alarmed to find it was a hundred and two. She
immediately rang Dr Mead and asked him to call as soon
as possible and then, with Mrs Bailey's help, re-made her
own bed with clean sheets and moved Adrian into it.

Only when all this had been completed did it occur to her
that his parents should be informed and she put through a
call to the hotel. It was explained to her that Mrs Marsh
was resting and had given strict orders that she was not
to be disturbed. Martha asked to speak to Mr Whitfield
instead and, after quite a lengthy interval, was told that
there was no reply from his room. Trembling with frus-
tration and anxiety, she stammered out a message, asking
one or other of them to call her back as soon as possible,
on a matter of extreme urgency.

It was Tim who answered this summons and he did not
sound particularly concerned when she gave him the news.

'Poor chap!' he said cheerfully. 'Probably picked up
some bug, I suppose.'

The doctor had visited Adrian in the mean time, bringing his usual magic dose of reassurance, so Martha was in
a more rational frame of mind and did not allow herself
to be annoyed by Tim's casual attitude.

'Dr Mead thinks it could be a virus infection. He's going to look in again this evening.'

'Jolly good! Sorry, Martha, must be a bit of a bore for you! Look, I tell you what. I'll give you a ring this evening and see what the form is.'

Martha took this airy promise with several grains of salt and was therefore all the more gratified when he not only did telephone again, just before dinner, but offered to present himself in the morning and sit with the patient for an hour or two, to give her a breather.

He was as good as his word, moreover, and arrived punctually at eleven o'clock, armed, somewhat surprisingly, with a game of Ludo, which he had bought at the village shop on his way. Either he had not noticed that Adrian was now seventeen, or else his own mental development had not progressed beyond the Ludo stage.

He was not totally devoid of sensitivity, however, and privately confided to Martha that Christine had refused to come.

'Between you and me, I believe she's afraid he may have something infectious. Well, she's got a lot to contend with at the moment, poor girl. Wouldn't do for her to go down with mumps or chicken-pox, on top of everything else. Still, we won't say anything about that to the lad, do you think? Wouldn't want to hurt his feelings. I'll just say she's feeling a bit off colour herself.'

He then breezed upstairs and into Martha's room, calling out, 'Well, and how's the invalid this fine morning?' for he was also a kindly man at heart, not given to threats or violence, if they could be avoided, and he was determined to see what could be done on a jolly, man-to-man basis, before resorting to sterner measures. Christine had not been in favour of this approach, dismissing it as a waste of time, but for once he had stood up to her and insisted that it was at least worth a try.

So, after the second game of Ludo, which Adrian had not troubled to disguise his ambition to lose with all possible speed, Tim embarked on the introductory phrases which he had been turning over in his mind ever since the first dice was thrown.

'Now, look here, old chap, I'm not going to read the riot act because the last thing I want is to come the heavy parent when you're feeling down in the mouth. So let's just get this business sorted out between ourselves and that'll be the end of it, eh? No punishments, no recriminations; all over and forgotten! What do you say?'

'I don't know what you're talking about,' Adrian muttered in a faint voice, turning very pale. He then flung himself back against the pillows and began to draw in heavy, sob-laden breaths.

Preening himself on having reduced the adversary to a pulp in the opening round, Tim said in a voice of quiet authority, 'I think you do, old man, and all I want is for you to tell me, without any frills or fibs, everything you know about that business on Sunday night.'

Unluckily for him, he had reckoned without the family weakness. In Tim's ears, the long, high wail which came soaring up from the pillows reminded him so forcibly of Christine at the height of her powers that he even had time to steel himself for the torrential hysterics which followed it. To Martha, called in to restore a degree of order into chaos, the scene was a carbon copy of dozens which she had lived through with Dolly.

Ten minutes later, chastened and subdued, Tim went on his way, irrevocably committed now to the procedure as laid down by Christine.

156

< 2 >

Billy's first shock came from arriving at the hotel at a quarter to one and finding Christine downstairs and waiting for him in the lounge. Those which followed were of a more nebulous character and arose chiefly from the fact that, during the ensuing twenty minutes, she not only pressed him to have a second drink, but, against all expectations, made no reference whatever to forged letters, practical jokes, or the little matter of a missing tape.

On the contrary, she had evidently invited him to lunch for the express purpose of cross-examining him on the subject of Daphne and the reasons for his marriage breaking up. This was not only mystifying, but tremendously boring as well, and he found it increasingly difficult to answer her silly questions, or even listen to them. So after a while he leant back and closed his eyes, while she burbled on about compatibility in general and the problems imposed by being tied to someone of inferior intelligence, in particular.

After a few minutes he opened his eyes again and said, 'I am sure you are right, Christine. After all, you've had more experience than the rest of us.'

She pursed her lips at this, but he did not notice, having already shut his eyes again. There followed another pause, in which he did some hard thinking, until it dawned on him that Christine had stopped talking, so he jogged her into action again by asking, 'Where is Tim, by the way?'

'Gone to see Adrian, who is ill in bed, as you probably know.'

'Yes, I do. What's the matter with him?'

'Oh, just flu, I imagine. Nothing serious, although Martha makes an almighty fuss, as you might expect. Tim thought he might be getting bored with all the female cosseting, so he went round to cheer him up.'

157

'How curious!'

'What's curious about it?'

'Well, he's never done so before, as far as I know.'

'Adrian hasn't been ill before.'

'As far as you know.'

'What a ridiculous thing to say! Of course I'd know.'

'I disagree.'

'Oh, for heaven's sake, Billy. You are in a foul mood today. And I thought this was going to be such fun! Why do we have to spend the whole time arguing about Adrian? Children of that age are so boring, don't you agree?'

'Not necessarily.'

'Well, perhaps girls are different. I never had any, thank God. Derek rather hankered for a big family, but the doctors absolutely warned me off having any more. One was bad enough. I nearly died with Adrian. Did you know that, Billy?'

'No.'

She spent five minutes telling him how she had nearly died with Adrian, in the course of which he did some more solid thinking. The next time he opened his eyes it was to say, 'Would you excuse me for a moment, Christine? I've just remembered that I promised to ring up a client. I may be able to catch him before he goes out to lunch.'

Without waiting for her consent, he got up and walked out of the room.

He did not need to look up the number and his call was answered on the second ring.

'Is Tim there, Martha?' he asked.

'No, my dear, I'm afraid not. He was here earlier on, you know, but he's gone now.'

'How long ago?'

'Oh, ages. More than an hour, I should think.'

'Thanks, Martha.'

'Is anything wrong?' she asked, but he did not hear her, having already replaced the receiver.

Nor did he waste time by ringing his own number, for, if his thinking had been right, he had an unpleasant feeling that Miranda would now be in a place where she could not hear the telephone.

Instead, and much to the astonishment of the head waiter, who had earlier received some very specific instructions from Christine, he marched straight through the restaurant, which had a separate entrance adjoining the car-park, got in his car and drove rapidly away.

< 3 >

Tim had also been cutting a few corners. His first thought, following his ignominious and premature retreat from Martha's cottage, was to restore his self-confidence and regroup his forces by downing a couple of doubles at the village pub. In fact, he had three because, when the second was finished, there still remained a hiatus to be filled before he could be reasonably certain that Billy would have left for his luncheon appointment. The result was that when he eventually went on his way to put phase two of the programme into operation, he was not only a little unsteady on his feet and uncoordinated in his movements, but quite disastrously over-confident.

More optimistic than ever of his ability to achieve his ends by peaceful, if not legitimate means, he parked his car about a hundred yards short of Billy's house and then walked along the lane to a section of the garden wall which had been partially knocked down by a swerving car during his undergraduate days and, as it turned out, had still not been built up again twenty-five years later.

In his somewhat euphoric state, he took this as a good omen, indicating that the gods fully approved of what he was up to and also that, if so much had remained unchanged, Billy's habits would not have altered either and that he would be able to enter the studio simply by turning the knob and walking inside.

Once again he was not disappointed and even the chaotic state of the interior did not daunt him for more than a brief flash. Optimism was soon restored by the reflection that, in fact, this was likely to make his task easier. Certainly, it could not fail to speed it up, for, he argued, though falsely as it happened, that, far from having to cover his tracks by replacing everything as he had found it, he could turn over every object in the room without anyone being the wiser.

His intention was to do precisely this before, as a last resort, moving on to the house proper and engaging in a battle of wits with Miranda, which had been second on the agenda. Unlike Christine, who was unable to believe that someone who had once loved her could ever break out of her thrall, he was thoroughly convinced that it was Billy himself who had organised the trick which had been played on them and that the object he sought must be hidden within yards of the spot where he now stood.

As it happened, he was right, but it was Miranda who overturned this relatively harmless programme. Having set aside the afternoon to give Adrian a driving lesson, she found herself at a loose end and, with idle hands and two hours to fill before her father returned, her mind naturally flew to work which he, above all, would have described as devilish. As soon as she had completed her daily stint of ballet exercises and eaten her own lunch, which consisted of a glass of milk and an apple, she armed herself with

160

cloths and brooms and a dustpan and brush and tripped off to spring-clean the studio.

Tim was crouching on the floor by the bookcase and had his back to her when she entered. The sound of the door opening brought his head round with a jerk, the book he had been holding slipped from his hands and, in the first flash of mutual recognition, it would have been hard to say which of them was the more scared.

Miranda was the first to achieve a semblance of recovery.

'What are you doing with my father's photograph album?' she demanded in a slightly quavering voice. 'Come to that, what are you doing here at all?'

Tim got to his feet, very deliberately brushing the dust from his knees and saying, in what he believed to be masterful tones, 'I have come here to fetch something and I think you know very well what it is.'

'I most certainly do not. You've no right to walk in here uninvited, so please go away at once.'

'Now, see here, young lady, you needn't come the innocent with me. I am quite sure you do know and I also believe you can tell me where I shall find it. I advise you to do so without delay. It will save us both a great deal of trouble. Come along, now! I don't want to hurt you, you must see that.'

'I haven't the faintest idea what you're talking about,' she said, though with less certainty now.

'Haven't you? Then may I ask why my boy, Adrian, went off into screaming hysterics when I mentioned it to him this morning?'

'Adrian?' she repeated. 'What's Adrian got to do with it?'

Her bewilderment was so patently genuine that his fraily based confidence oozed away and he began to bluster.

161

'Stop playing the fool, do you hear me? I mean to get it, whatever tricks you may try, and I've no time for silly games.'

'Neither have I, and if you don't leave this instant, I shall call the police.'

'Oh no, you won't,' he said, and made a clumsy dive to get between her and the door.

Miranda had seen it coming and she dropped the broom across his path, so that he tripped over it, staggered and only just saved himself from falling. By the time he regained his balance she had planted herself with her back against the door, and she remained there, determined and implacable, even though she could see from his suffused face and bulging eyes that he was now beside himself with rage.

'Now, which is it to be?' she asked. 'Are you going to leave quietly, or — ' then ducked with the speed of lightning as his hand came swinging up to strike her.

Billy was out of breath too when he kicked open the door and plunged into the studio, and what little of it remained was instantly taken away by the sight which confronted him. Tim was lying on the floor, apparently unconscious, his wrists and ankles bound with check dusters, and Miranda was calmly stacking up the loose papers on his drawing-board.

'What the hell is going on?' he demanded in querulous tones, hardly knowing what to complain about first.

'Ah! Caught in the act! I didn't expect you quite so soon,' Miranda admitted. 'All things considered, though, I'm glad you're here. I didn't like to leave him while I went to call the police, in case he came to and managed to untie himself. All the junk you clutter this place up with, and not a length of rope anywhere! Not even a key to the door!'

'I keep that in my pocket, naturally,' he explained, 'but this is hardly the time to be discussing such matters. How does this creature come to be lying on my floor?'

'Me and my karate lessons. I should think my teacher will be pleased when I tell him how handy they were. And I finished him off with the back of the carpet brush. I fancy I may have concussed him, but I don't think they can charge me with grievous bodily harm, because it was self-defence. I really and truly believe he was going to beat me up.'

'I shouldn't be at all surprised.'

'Oh? Perhaps I've been rather lucky, then?'

'On the whole, Miranda, I should say you had. He has quite an unsavoury record.'

FRIDAY, 31st AUGUST

Robert Meyer was so often away from home, on mentionable and unmentionable business, that Avril had made a corner in unattached men and Billy Jones and Tubby Wiseman were two of her favourites. On the last evening in August she had invited them both, which, with Martha and herself, made a cosy little party round the dinner table, 'specially as they all shared a burning interest in the principal topic of conversation. In the main, though, it was Tubby who dominated the scene, with the others dutifully playing out their minor roles.

'The day the poor chap decided to throw in the sponge and sell up his estate was the day he signed his own death warrant,' he announced somewhat portentously, looking with respect at his glass of wine, from which he had just inhaled the first exploratory sniff. 'Up till then the other two had been managing very well on his income and the capital was tied up safe and sound. And the sad part of it is that it was the last thing he wanted. Africa had always been his home and he dreaded having to leave and settle in an alien land.'

'So why did he consent to go?' Avril asked.

'Mrs Marsh persuaded him. She saw which way the wind was blowing and realised it was inevitable that the estate would be nationalised eventually, probably with inadequate compensation to the owners, and she wasn't having any of that. I dare say Marsh would have been

164

content to jog along under the new regime and salvage what he could, but that wasn't nearly enough for her. She wanted to sell out for the highest price they could get and go while the going was good.'

'That sounds all too typical,' Martha admitted sadly. 'In fact, it was more or less what she told me herself. But how did she get round Derek, I wonder, if he was really so unwilling to leave?'

'I think it was mainly by infiltrating the idea that their lives were in danger. Mind you, I'm sure that side of it was grossly exaggerated, if not pure invention, but she put it about that their own servants were turning insolent and hostile and even that she was beginning to have fears for her own safety. Naturally, that would have worried Marsh more than anything.'

'I think she had a stroke of luck, too, in that respect,' Billy said. 'From something Miranda told me, it appears that she left her safe door open one night and some money was stolen from it. She blamed it on one of the servants, wrongly, as I happen to know, but when he was questioned about it he lost his nerve and ran away. A small thing on its own, but no doubt it served to fan the flames and weaken Derek's resistance.'

'And do you honestly believe that incident was just a matter of luck?' Tubby asked him. 'Begging your pardon, Martha! Perhaps one shouldn't be discussing your relations quite so freely, but, from what I've heard of a certain young gentleman, I should guess that Mrs Marsh was perfectly well aware that there was someone on the premises that evening who could be relied upon to help himself from an open safe.'

'No need to spare my feelings, Tubby. You have every justification for saying that, as I know all too well. The only objection is that the servant did run away, which

165

might be taken as an admission of guilt, so perhaps we are being unfair to Adrian this time.'

Billy refrained from comment, but Tubby was not so squeamish.

'I can well imagine that she nagged the servant about it to the extent that, however accustomed to her scenes and complaints, he was so worn down that it needed only one mild enquiry from the master himself to convince the chap that his days were numbered, however innocent he might be. However, his running away was certainly a stroke of luck for Mrs Marsh and Whitfield, in the sense that it set the pattern for their next little scheme.'

'Which was?'

'To murder Marsh in his office.'

'But Tubby, my dear!'

'Yes, yes, I know what you're going to say, Martha, but just bear with me for a while. It is important to remember that, as soon as Marsh had signed away the deeds and got the maximum price for the estate, he was to be disposed of with the least possible delay. There were obviously numerous reasons for this and perhaps the main one was that it would be easier to get away with it out there than in this country. There really had been some isolated, but genuine attacks on white men by extremists or guerrilla fighters and naturally they were hoping to gain every advantage they could from this well-known fact.'

'Yes, but all the same, Tubby . . .'

'I know, I know, but just let me finish. I think another reason for their being in such a hurry was because, as soon as Derek's capital was released, they became desperately worried as to what he might do with it. For all I know, there may have been the added incentive that, if his death had occurred in Africa, his widow would only

166

have been liable for the death duties of that country, which are probably a drop in the ocean compared to our own. There hasn't been time to go into that aspect, but I do feel certain that the longer Marsh remained alive the greater was the risk of his fortune being dissipated before they could get their hands on it. Mrs Marsh went flat out in blaming her own tight-fistedness on her husband. She told everyone how excessively mean he was, but all of us here know it was simply not true and, in fact, I think they had good cause for wanting to hurry things along because there can be little doubt that, if he'd lived for another six months, he might well have parted with half his capital.'

'Yes, I realise that and, as you know, I'm in a particularly strong position to confirm everything you say,' Martha said despairingly, 'but if you'd only let me get a word in edgeways, there is something I must point out. It wasn't Derek who was attacked in his office, it was Tim.'

'Ah! And there's an interesting point. You knew that because Mrs Marsh had referred to it in a letter, where one is naturally more deliberate in one's phrasing; but when she first mentioned it to me she had got rather carried away and, in describing the incident, she spoke of "my husband" having been the victim. It wasn't until later that I discovered that in fact the victim was Whitfield. Well now, I can thoroughly understand that there might have been times when she became a little confused as to which one she was currently married to, but thinking back it seemed to me much more likely that her mistake was due to a slip of a different nature. In other words, it was her subconscious mind which trapped her into referring to "my husband", for the simple reason that the attack had been designed for him. Later on, I learnt from another source that Whitfield had been assaulted and injured and that was when I became satisfied in my own mind that they were in it together and that Marsh was their target.'

'But Tim was quite seriously hurt. Are you suggesting that his injuries were self-inflicted?'

'No, Martha, I am not. Am I permitted to give you a reconstruction of the event?'

'Yes, Tubby, you are,' Avril told him. 'You are so good at reconstructing. It is one of your great talents . . . '

'Just as choosing wine is one of yours. May I help myself to a little more of this excellent Pontet-Canet?'

'Pray do, although the compliment should go to Robert.'

After an interval, Tubby continued.

'So picture, if you will, a lush green tea plantation in the heart of Africa and in the centre of it an old, colonial-style building in which are situated the offices of both Marsh and Whitfield. At the time we are speaking of there are lights in the upper storey, but the ground floor is in semi-darkness. We can tell from this that it is getting on for seven o'clock and, as the daylight begins to fade, the workers are drifting in from the fields towards the various huts where they will deposit the day's crop and collect their wages.

'One figure detaches himself from the rest, walks rapidly towards the office building and disappears inside. He has short, curly, grizzled hair and is wearing khaki shorts and tennis shoes. In the half-light he could easily be mistaken for one of the labourers and, just to complete the picture, he is carrying a crude agricultural tool, something on the lines of a pickaxe, which is still used in those parts by small-holders and farm workers. However, he is not one of them, he is Tim Whitfield and he moves swiftly and silently towards the stairs and begins to mount them. Unknown to him . . .'

Tubby paused at this point, for further refreshment and to select his words for the next instalment.

'Unknown to him, there is an equally silent watcher. A man has entered the building a few seconds after him, a white-robed figure, wearing a scarlet cummerbund and a scarlet tarboosh on his head. His name is Joshua and he really is an African.

'Seeing this figure on the stairs, Joshua has but one thought and, in view of some recent upheavals in his country, it is a logical one. He concludes without hesitation that here is some villain who has been sent to murder the master, the man whose family have sheltered and cared for Joshua all his life and for whom he has nothing but love and respect. So what does he do?'

'I can't wait to hear,' Avril confessed, 'but before you tell us I am bound to say that I think you invented the last bit. I don't see how you could know.'

'I maintain that a certain licence is permissible on an informal occasion of this sort and the fact is that he acted with the utmost courage and resolution. So it is fair to say that he had enough love and respect for his employer not to stand by and see him clobbered with a pickaxe. You could add that he acted with rather too much courage and resolution for his own good, for it was not until he had flung himself on the intruder, seized the weapon from him and started hacking out in all directions that he realised that this was not an intruder at all, but Mr Whitfield, the manager of the estate.'

'Whereupon, he lost his head, dropped the weapon and bolted? Is that it?'

'Quite so,' Tubby agreed, looking faintly put out by Avril's succinct résumé of an occurrence which he could doubtless have stretched over four sentences. 'Exactly so. Leaving Whitfield in a state of disarray, with a wounded

169

right arm and therefore in no position to carry out the rest of the evening's programme.'

'I want you all to know that I am not defending my cousin, or Tim either,' Martha said, 'but, since this is largely guesswork, how can you be sure that it happened in the way you have described and not in the way they have claimed? I mean, what was Joshua doing in the office building, anyway?'

'He had been sent there by Mrs Marsh, ostensibly to deliver a message to her husband about a change in their dinner arrangements. I should guess it was the kind of thing that often happened, wouldn't you? After the office staff had packed up there was no one on the switchboard and it seems reasonable to suppose that neither Marsh nor Whitfield would have bothered to have an outside line switched through to their offices, with so much cheap human labour at their disposal. I dare say it was quite a routine affair for Joshua to go running back and forth with messages. On this particular occasion, however, we may take it that the real purpose of his errand was to ensure his being seen in the vicinity of the crime at the appropriate time. And he would have been seen, there is no question about that. His uniform was so distinctive, for one thing, quite unlike the clothes worn by the plantation workers; and, with all of them beginning to move towards the exit gate, he would have stood out like a windmill on a flat landscape. It had all been carefully and cleverly planned.'

'Nevertheless, it didn't come off,' Avril remarked. 'How was that? Did Joshua suspect some dirty work at the crossroads?'

'Oh no, positively not. Mrs Marsh had sent him out of the house at a time which would ensure his arriving at the office at, let us say, twenty minutes to seven, but just

170

before this Whitfield had made some excuse to go outside and engage in some conflab with one of the overseers. At a few minutes before seven o'clock, when Joshua is reckoned to be safely on his way home again, Whitfield intends to return to the building, having armed himself with a pickaxe, creep upstairs to Marsh's office, strike him down from behind and then raise the alarm. Mrs Marsh would subsequently deny ever having sent Joshua anywhere at all, which puts the poor devil in a proper jam. Even the total absence of his prints on the weapon is no help to him because all the house servants are supplied with white cotton gloves, which they are required to wear for certain of their duties.'

'Oh dear,' Martha said, the depth of her distress reducing her to utter bathos. 'Oh dear, that wasn't a very nice thing to do, was it? I mean, that poor, innocent man, who'd worked hard for them for all those years! How ever could they have been so wicked and callous?'

'Hard to say, but, if it's any consolation to you, things didn't turn out so badly for him as they'd planned. Luckily, man is never perfect and very few of his plots and schemes are either. Various human weaknesses caused this one to go awry. Mrs Marsh had over-estimated her own ability to make everyone jump to it every time she opened her mouth. No doubt she had given Joshua strict instructions to go straight there and back, and don't dilly-dally on the way, but, although she is shrewd up to a point, she lacks imagination and I dare say she had not bothered to invent any plausible message for him to deliver. And Joshua may also have had his little failings. Realising quite well that there could be no urgency about it, he would have seen no harm in stopping on the way to chat to a friend, or to rest up for a bit in the porter's lodge. But whatever the cause, we know that he entered the office building nearly half an hour after the appointed time and we know what resulted. Once he discovered that the man he'd intercepted so courageously was really Mr Whitfield in semi-disguise, he didn't stop to argue; he made off before they could catch him. And he got a good start because Whitfield was in such a state of pain and shock that he passed out. It was probably twenty minutes or so before Marsh came out of his office and found him on the stairs.

'So, you see, the plot misfired, but all was by no means lost. No one questioned Whitfield's version of the incident and Joshua wasn't around to defend himself. Best of all, Derek Marsh had not the least suspicion that his old friend had set out to club him to death. However, they naturally couldn't use the same dodge twice and, as soon as the last formalities were out of the way and the money handed over, they lit out for England, home and beauty. And we all know what happened when they got here. Presumably it was Dolly's accident which set their minds working along those lines.'

'I must be getting feeble-minded,' Martha complained, 'and I know poor Derek wasn't very bright either, but I still don't understand how they persuaded him to go to an appointment an hour ahead of the time he'd fixed for himself. And even if they did, he surely wasn't such a ninny as to stand by while Tim cut the staircase away and then obediently get into position at the top of it?'

'No, he wasn't,' Tubby agreed, 'and the answer to that puzzle hinges largely on a telephone call. Shall I tell them, Bill, or will you?'

'Oh, you, by all means,' Billy said.

'To be precise, then, the telephone call in which Marsh put the Sunday morning appointment forward to twelve-fifteen. Only, as it happens, he didn't do anything of the kind. He was not even in the room at the time. It

172

was a tape-recording of his voice, made two weeks earlier in a London hotel.'

'Got it!' Avril exclaimed, sitting bolt upright and snapping her fingers. 'And, funnily enough, I smelt a rat when Martha told me about Christine buying that expensive present for Adrian. I concluded it was a bribe to get him to go and stay with his country cousins, but one should always back one's hunches. How on earth did you find out, Billy?'

'I can take no credit for it. It was simply my capacity for storing up useless information. It operates on every level, you know. I'd been looking through an old photograph album and I came across one of Tim and Christine and myself standing on the steps of the Madeleine. We'd been to a service there. Tim wanted to go because he'd told us it was his saint's day. I missed the connection, at first. You have to remember that this was twenty-five years ago. But then Miranda told me about the recording machine which Christine was guarding like a jealous gorgon and I recalled a remark which Derek had made on the telephone, that they were going to church because it was Tim's saint's day. The bells eventually began to ring and I checked the date of the Paris photograph. Sure enough, there was a discrepancy of two weeks.'

Tubby did not look best pleased at being edged out of the limelight and took up the tale again with all speed.

'Fortunately for us, the Marshes knew so few people in England that it did not take us long to trace the original call. In fact, he was speaking to his lawyer, Charles Lawson, who lives in Kew and had invited them all to lunch on their first Sunday in London. They were discussing what time he should drive to their hotel to collect them and Whitfield and Mrs Marsh had made a point of preparing the ground so that Marsh would use all the necessary

173

phrases. This was their first step in constructing an alibi and, when the time came to make use of it, all they had to do was to insert some of these recorded remarks into the conversation she had a fortnight later with Billy.'

'So poor Derek had no idea the appointment had been changed and went off like a lamb to the slaughter at eleven o'clock?'

'Yes, indeed, and Whitfield too. It gave him a full hour to work in, more than enough to trick Marsh into investigating some phenomenon behind the door at the head of the old staircase; and also to deal with the telephone wires, after making sure that his old friend was well and truly dead.'

'I am sorry to keep raising the same point,' Martha said, 'but even with all that time to spare, I still can't understand how Tim could have removed a whole section of the staircase with Derek looking on.'

'He didn't have to. All that had been prepared in advance.'

'But when?'

'On Saturday afternoon, some time between four-thirty and five. We can fix it as accurately as that because we know when he left the London hotel and the next person to see him was yourself, Martha, when he was driving away from Bookers Farm, on his way back to London to collect Mrs Marsh and wearing the simplest of all disguises, namely a chauffeur's peaked cap, pulled well forward. The lady passenger on the back seat was a pillow, with one of Christine's new hats pinned on to it.'

'But Tubby, my dear, it must have been almost five o'clock when I saw the car and I thought it had been proved up to the hilt that they were both in the theatre from a quarter to five onwards.'

'I know. It was a sort of conjuring trick, really, and we

174

were looking in the wrong direction. I should have seen through it sooner, and so might Frank, I suppose, but we got there in the end.'

'I think what we badly need at this point is another reconstruction, so that you can explain to us how Tim contrived to be in two places at once.'

'Simplest thing in the world, which is probably why we were so nearly taken in. You see, Frank got a clear identification of Tim at the dress shop, so we knew, without the shadow of a doubt, that he'd been there until after one o'clock. It wasn't even necessary to get a description from the people at the hotel because, naturally, they knew him well and referred to him by name. So by this time we had established the idea that he and Mrs Marsh were together, but, although it's true that they were, up to the time when they left the hotel, they separated immediately afterwards. When Christine bobbed up again at the theatre she was still with a man, but it wasn't the same one. Unfortunately, in tracking their movements, we had concentrated on getting descriptions of Mrs Marsh, who was far and away the more outstanding in appearance and personality, and they were authentic down to the last eyelash. But when Frank went back to the theatre a few days later he took along a couple of photographs. One was of Whitfield and the other a character named Jim McBean. It was Lawson who tipped us off about him, incidentally. We got a notion of how the trick might have been played and we thought Lawson might have been the man at the theatre. He was able to prove us wrong and he came up with McBean as the only close friend the Marshes had in this country. He was just the innocent tool, poor fellow, quite unaware that he was providing an alibi for a murderer, but when the barmaid was shown the two photographs she had no hesitation in picking out McBean as the man who had bought the champagne. It was the one really bad mistake that Mrs Marsh made, but perhaps we shouldn't be too critical. It's possible that he ordered it without even consulting her.'

'Well, I know one ought not to want wicked people to go unpunished,' Martha said, 'but I can't pretend to be glad about this. It seems so hard on poor little Adrian. He's not an easy character, but is it any wonder? Just think what he must have inherited from that pair!'

'I shouldn't worry too much about Adrian,' Billy said, briefly opening his eyes. 'His heredity may not be so desperate as you imagine.'

'I shouldn't think they come much worse,' Avril remarked.

'Well, on one side, admittedly. That's to say, you only have to look at him to realise he's Christine's son, but he doesn't take after Tim in any way at all. In fact, if you think of it dispassionately, there's a much closer resemblance to Derek. Repressed, self-conscious, inarticulate; they're all words which apply equally to both of them.'

'Well, I never did! I wonder if you could be right, Billy.'

'I can point to another characteristic in common, if you need one. Just think for a moment!'

There was a short silence and then Avril shook her head.

'I have thought, but it's done me no good. I can't find a single one.'

'No? Then how about that compulsion to load people with expensive presents? It's so strong in Adrian that it's turned him into a thief. On the other hand, it can be an endearing quality, when kept in check. I dare say Adrian won't turn out too badly, if we all pull together.'

'So let us now drink to that pious hope,' Tubby said, pouring himself the last drop from the decanter.